The Black Bitch and Other Stories

The Black Bitch and Other Stories

P. Raja

DIVE IN THE OCEAN OF KNOWLEDGE
Ocean Books

Ocean Books Pvt. Ltd.
ISO 9001:2008 Publishers

Published by
Ocean Books (P) Ltd.
4/19 Asaf Ali Road,
New Delhi-110 002 (INDIA)
e-mail: info@oceanbooks.in

ISBN 978-81-8430-337-7
THE BLACK BITCH AND OTHER STORIES
by P. Raja

Edition
First, 2016

Price
₹ 250.00 (Rupees Two Hundred Fifty only)

Printed at
Yash Printographics, Noida

For my friends
R. David and R. Marimouthou

Acknowledgements

All the short stories in this collection made their first round through **All India Radio, Pondicherry**. I am thankful to its Director for floating them in AIR.

I am thankful also to the **editors** of the following newspapers, magazines and journals, and e-magazines for publishing these stories:

The Statesman (8th Day), Kolkata
The Statesman Festival Annual, Kolkata
Rock Pebbles, Odisha
The Light of Andamans, Port Blair
Kalatarangam, Lakshadweep
Contemporary Vibes, Chandigarh
Indian Book Chronicle, Jaipur
Labyrinth, Gwalior
Poets International, Bengaluru
Samas, Odisha
Muse India
Creative Saplings

I am thankful to M/s **Ocean Books**, New Delhi for gathering these stories between covers.

Special thanks are owed to **Dr. D. Gnanasekaran**, an authority on ELT and Indian Writing in English, for writing an 'Afterword' to this collection.

Above all, I am extremely grateful to **Prof. Manoj Das,** who right from the beginning of my writing career took my hand in his and guided me into the world of publishing.

Contents

A Disease of the Mind

Poor Seena! She could not even close her eyes that night. She was both happy and unhappy – happy because her physician had given the good news of her becoming a mother for a second time; unhappy because her husband Vasan was not in favour of it.

Vasan's reasons were genuine. When the physician congratulated him, his face fell for fear that his little darling Aruna would be upset over the arrival of a newcomer, who would share her parents' affection.

Around midnight, Seena switched on the overhead light. The whole bedroom budded into view. To her left was her husband, a supine figure on the bed. And to her right, a little cherub, half clad, her wee hand hugging tight her mother's belly.

Seena half sat up. Aruna's hand slipped slowly down. But her mother's movements did not disturb her deep sleep. Heaving a sigh of relief, Seena shook her husband awake.

Vasan woke up with a start. He squeezed his eyelids and blinked a while. It took minutes for him to come back to himself. "Are you still awake?" he asked his wife.

"Your words have killed my sleep," she said, "You know about me very well. I do not get sleep till my problems get solved."

Vasan slapped his forehead twice cursing his fate. "What is your problem?" he asked and pretended to be cool.

"Hm… You pinch the baby and rock its cradle too… I know you are an adept at it," Seena said with a wry smile.

"Look Seena dear! No wind wafts problems into our home and for that matter into nobody's home. We people create problems for ourselves and get entangled in them and find no way out. I only warned you of the mental health of our daughter. Aruna is still a baby and as a first born, she enjoys our love and affection. Imagine her plight at the arrival of an unexpected newcomer." Vasan heaved a sigh.

"As if this is not happening anywhere else!" Seena expressed every word with a grudge.

"Let us not argue over it. I told you only to postpone it till our little darling is mature enough to welcome the newborn with open arms."

"Oh! That will take another ten years…You want me to wait for ten more years. I would have grown older by ten years. And how fertile my womb would be at that time, nobody would ever know. You will never know how excruciating the pangs of labour would be in my middle age…"

Vasan leaned back against a pillow and stretched himself on the bed. "And so…?" he asked, his eyes staring into space.

"You philosophised so much on problems. I too have something to contribute to it. What sounds a small problem for you may emerge very big to me. And for yet another, it may not be a problem at all. Better leave the problem to me," Seena said all the time admiring her husband's portrait-like posture.

"Oh…dear!…dear! Please try to understand me. My intention is not to harass you. I want peace to prevail in our home. The newcomer will definitely upset Aruna. And we will directly or indirectly be responsible for it."

"Well dear! I am ready to abort the child, only if you promise to carry my child in your womb after ten years…. So that you will know what birth pangs are," Seena said and looked for Vasan's reaction.

Vasan broke into a guffaw. Seena was delighted to see him laugh. She knew for sure that laughter was the best medicine that cured all diseases of the mind. He too knew that Seena was good at putting things behind her. They went right back to normal after that bickering.

The fact that they kept their voices down so as not to wake Aruna, showed the affection both of them had for their only child.

Who would have imagined that something like this could happen in spite of all the precautions they took? And yet right now, even as they speak, similar things are happening all around the world. There are plenty of stories like this in the hospital. But no doctor tells them out.

Laughing made them forget about everything. They lapsed into silence and when the morning sun pushed them from darkness to light, they found themselves in each other's arms. Child Aruna, unaware of what was happening around slept peacefully.

Peace was restored. Seena was profusely thankful to her husband for his patient hearing. Yet the doubt raised by Vasan began to dominate her mind.

She should keep her word by hook or by crook. But how to? Monotheist she was, Seena never wasted her time in temples nor had a pooja room in her house. Her God was her Conscience. "Who could be a better God than one's own conscience?" That is her philosophy of life. This time too her conscience found for her a way out.

One evening when Aruna called her mother to the backyard of the house to play, Seena jumped at the opportunity.

While they were at play, Seena said casually of the importance of having a playmate in one's own house.

"Yes, Amma! Chitra, our next door girl, has a brother and a sister to play with. But it is a pity that I don't have any," said Aruna.

"Don't you want one?" Seena queried sharply.

"Yes, Amma! What should I do to get one?" Aruna demanded, her eyes glinting.

"Simply pray with me."

Aruna squirmed. "I don't know what you're talking about. I asked Chitra's mother the very same question. She said, 'Your mama and papa should work for it'."

"Oh, dear! She has put it differently," Seena said dismissively. She added, "Your papa and I have prayed enough for your playmate. And now it is your turn. You should pray if you want to have one."

"But I have never seen you and papa pray for my playmate," Aruna said innocently.

"Of course, every night," Seena said with a giggle, "when you are fast asleep. We didn't want you to hear."

"Where did you both pray?"

"On the terrace."

"To what God?"

While Seena fumbled for an answer, Aruna shot her next question. "Our neighbours keep their gods in their pooja rooms. But you don't have even one in any of our rooms. To whom did you pray?"

"Don't you know, darling, that there is only one God who takes care of us all? He is in the Heavens. It is the sky. Your papa and I prayed to Him from the terrace of our house."

As though reading her mother's mind, Aruna interrupted her thoughts. "God is omnipotent and omniscient. You can pray to Him anywhere, any time and your prayer will be answered."

"Aha…aha...Excellent! My cute little angel! Where did you learn all these?"

"My papa once told me when I asked him what is inside a temple. He took me inside the temple once and showed all the stone dolls, life size."

Seena shrugged her shoulders. She thought that the topic of bringing a playmate to Aruna would make her look like a lost child. But the child's reactions were unexpected. She thanked her husband in her heart of hearts and said to herself: "Harvesting has begun."

For a moment, there was silence, followed by a long exhalation of breath from the back of a four-wheeler.

"Papa…Papa has come back from office," Aruna yelled and ran towards Vasan getting down from his car.

"I am going to have a playmate very soon, Papa," Aruna said in all glee.

Vasan was taken aback. He looked askance at Seena. She laughed at his bewilderment.

That night, after a very sumptuous dinner of fish curry, rice and deep fried prawns, all three of them climbed the stairs that led to the terrace.

The sky was bright with the moon. There were winking eyes all over.

"Now is the time to pray. God is all eyes and so all ears," said Seena. "No, no, no…You don't have to kneel down to pray. God does not want anyone to be uncomfortable when people throw open their hearts."

Aruna stood up and stood between her parents.

Seena said, "Now repeat all that I say. Pray only once with all your mind and heart to get your desires fulfilled."

"Only once, Amma!"

"Yes, only once but everyday till your prayer is answered."

"What should I say, Amma?"

"Listen carefully and repeat: 'Oh, Almighty god! Give me a brother or a sister to be my own playmate. Life is dull without a brother or a sister. Please answer my prayer as early as you can'."

Aruna prayed. She prayed every night for a brother or a sister.

One day Seena said showing all her teeth: "Aruna, darling! Your prayer is answered." She then took Aruna's hand into hers and placed the palm of her wee hand against her bulging tummy.

Aruna felt something inside her mom's belly move. "What is it?" she asked.

"Your playmate has arrived. Your prayer is answered."

"Is it a brother or a sister?" Aruna asked beaming with joy.

"You'll have to wait for a few more months. You want a brother or a sister?"

"Both," Aruna said with her eyes gleaming. "Two playmates. Why should I have one when Chitra has two?"

That night, Aruna stood amidst her parents, and prayed: "Oh, almighty God! Give me a brother and a sister to be my own playmates. Life is dull without a brother and a sister. Please answer my prayer as early as you can."

Listening to her prayer, bewildered Vasan said, "My goodness, she is right. What do we do?"

Seena gripped her husband's hand tighter and whispered, "Don't know."

□

Ahalya's Curse

Before you decide to curse me, let me have your audience. Cursed be me if I fail to convince you. If you feel convinced, then leave me to myself. To live with you or go with Lord Indran is my concern.

O Sage! You brought me up. You sincerely and wholeheartedly fulfilled the wishes of Brahma, who entrusted me to you. I am grateful to you as a daughter would to her father. You were a mother too to me, for I have learnt to distinguish between affection and love. You taught me everything that an impartial guru would to his illustrious disciple.

You should have stopped there, O Sage! You should have stopped there. It is out of greed you played the fourth role. It is unexpected of you. All calamities in life are caused by greed. Greed is the offspring of overconfidence. We develop this sort of confidence once we fail to understand our limitations.

Not knowing one's limitations is a sin... an unpardonable one at that. You married me.

What if Brahma had given me as your bride? You could have easily rejected the offer had you put your common sense to use. Why do you men lose all your senses when it comes to a woman?

Sages like you are revered everywhere. People pedestal you in their hearts and worship you. They consider you as an intermediary between God and Man. They think you are wise. Yet how shamelessly you fall for women!

Brahma created me. You nourished me. What are you both to me if not fathers? None of you ever seemed to have any respect for the woman in me. To both of you, I should have looked like a commodity. A commodity can never have any opinion of its own. And so both of you never bothered about my wishes. And your decisions were final.

Brahma if asked would have given a slippery answer: Where can I find for you a better being than Gowthama? You for your turn would have said: you will be safe in my hands.

I became your wife. Rather I was made your wife even before I could ask myself whether I liked it or not. Such a thing happens to ninety per cent of women in our country. It is destined so perhaps. Or is it a curse on our motherland?

Brahma made you happy by advising you to marry me. You made Brahma happy by obeying him. To you he is the Guru. And Guru's words are law. To him you are the best among Sages. He had two birds by flinging a single stone. You had two mangoes in a single shot.

Neither of you seemed to care a hay for me. The butcher made the eater happy. The eater made the butcher happy. But where did the lamb disappear?

The poor lamb has lost its identity. From lovely lamb to meat, from mutton to food, from delectable dish to faeces and from foul smelling faeces to earth again.

In the case of the helpless lamb, it had the satisfaction of becoming food for someone who appreciated it as it melted on one's tongue. But me? Sage Gowthama's wife... That's how the world began to identify me. I was Ahalya no more. From childhood to girlhood, from girlhood to wifehood, from wifehood to motherhood, from motherhood to ... Oh! The several hoods of women, they are destined to pass before they become dust with dust.

Brahma gave a body to my soul. He gave me to you. But you saw only the soul and ignored the body.

I am Brahma's daughter. I am beauty incarnate. I am special to the great creator. He told me once that he made much use of sandal paste to mould my body.

O Sage! Have you ever looked at me at close quarters? Who in all the seven worlds has such a shapely and well-chiselled nose as mine?

It is the nose that speaks for the face. And mine is the most beautiful one. It is unique in its own way.

Have you ever noticed my eyes… my swimming eyes? What beauty in any part of the world has them?

Well? I am a stupid woman talking of beauty to you. All my words will sound nonsensical to you. When you can't even see and admire my face, which is an open book, what use can there be if I speak of the hidden treasures that my father took pains to bless me with?

Devas and Asuras would have vied with each other to sing of my frame in glorifying terms. Poetasters too would have come out with genuine lines of pure poetry.

A good woman inspires a man; a brilliant one interests him; a beautiful one fascinates him; a sympathetic one gets him. I know I am all the four rolled into one. Yet I failed to get you.

I spent several days, months, and then years in trying to know the root of my failure. Then one day I understood that it was not my failure. It dawned on me that you are not a man.

It was a late realisation, of course. You have no feeling for me. Fine! But you have no feeling for any other woman too.

Perhaps you have outgrown all such human feelings, which you would call human weakness. This is one solid case in which body magnetism failed. One who has conquered all his senses can never be a man.

In all these years of married life, I've been living just like a stone, a dead wood. I doubt if you ever knew what a wretched life I was leading even when you are alive and kicking. It was a death-in-life existence.

I needed a saviour, who could look at me with lust-filled eyes. This is what every woman worth her salt ever wants her man to do. It is only lust that leads to love, and never love to lust.

Lust is the essence of life… the only means of satisfying the biological urge. Without it there can be no creation. Brahma would have to sit idle only to be forgotten once and for all.

Indran, the lustful lad of the firmament, is really my prayer answered.

Just try to recollect what happened in the morning, a short while ago. I know you are not in that mood now. So, I will do that for you.

The cock crowed. You woke up. You went out to take your morning bath. You never knew that you were tricked by a human voice. People call you sage. But how gullible are you?

I knew it. I knew it was not a rooster's voice. I was also certain that my saviour had come.

A few days ago when I was half clad and bathing in the river, Indran speeding in his vehicle amidst the clouds eyed me and slowed down. I waved my hand smiling at him all the time. He too smiled back and disappeared.

The next day when I was bathing, I heard a voice from behind the bushy trees that said: no tongue can paint your beauty.

I was happy at heart. I jumped for joy. All because someone has seen me and found that I am a beauty beyond words. Neither a lexicographer nor a fertile poet can ever express in words the joy I experienced at that hour on that day.

I looked around and asked who is it. Indran showed up as if he were waiting for my words of permission.

I smiled. My long tresses were hiding the front of my body and I didn't make any attempt to hide them with my hands. Neither did I go down into the water. Instead I stood knee deep.

Indran came closer to me on the bank. His words told me that I am tall and graceful and that my magnificent hair cascades in profusion from my shapely head.

Beneath my arching eyebrows, I learnt only from him that my eyes like twin stars shine forth with a brilliancy only softened by long, black, curving lashes that veil them.

It is not that I do not know how delicately and finely my features are moulded. But when he continued I fell in love with myself. He spoke at length of the winning sweetness of my smile and certified that the tender lines of my lovely mouth personify the gentleness of my nature.

He was all praise for my complexion. Deliciously creamy, he said, with a transparent yet perfectly healthy texture that never wearies one's eyes and becomes insipid.

He stopped awhile as I admired him and his words of praise. He stepped into the water and embraced me.

It was really a man's touch, a touch I was craving for all along. He brushed my long tresses aside and I didn't object to it. He saw the real me, unadulterated and uncivilised. He closed his eyes for a few seconds or so and heaved a sigh.

I reciprocated his sigh and expressed my longing for man's touch. Why should I die a virgin and allow the worms to try my long preserved virginity?

My heart pounded for him. He was the first man to see my beautiful frame with nothing on it. My soul accepted him as my true husband. My body craved to consummate.

But the bank of the river can never be the right place to consummate. And we are not animals in heat. Above all, my conscience, the inner voice, warned me that someone might be looking.

So, I gave Indran the ruse. I told him to come well before dawn and park his vehicle away from your sight. It was I who told him to imitate a rooster at that odd hour. It was I who advised him to make the best use of this hour for consummation.

Oh God! Indran is a real man. He showed me the woman-power in me, which you allowed to slumber. But for Indran, I would have died an untimely death. Thanks to my Lord.

You can never, O sage, brand me unchaste. I slept with only one man. I will sleep only with him. I would say I am made for him. If Indran happens to die, I would love to jump into his funeral pyre.

Do not brand me faithless. There is no frailty in my act. And I am not perfidious.

So, think twice before you curse me. A chaste woman like me can also curse and her curse is as good or as bad as any Sage's.

Aren't you listening? Oh God! You are already a stone.

□

Pousse-Pousse

A lonely sultry afternoon drove me into the museum. I have never visited one before in my two score and twelve years of my sojourn on Planet Earth.

It is not that I am a stranger to museums. I had spent several precious hours inside the museums of Chennai, Kolkata, and Trivandrum not with any purpose of gathering historical knowledge but with the ulterior mctive of whiling away the time. I had the opportunity of staying in these places at the expense of the academies that sponsored my trip as a writer. Most of these sessions unfortunately fell in summer and summer is summer wherever we are in India, unless we reach heights.

I found not much difference between one museum and the other for they invariably spoke in silence for the glory of our past. Cultural heritage, spiritual heritage, literary heritage, historical heritage, political heritage and God knows what other heritage do these places of interest display for their interested, disinterested and uninterested visitors. Most of the rooms in these museums stink of bat turd, the only thing not known of in history books. I have seen several people throw up in such rooms and thereby create a mess of that place preventing others from entry.

These purported to be well maintained, but, in fact, ill-maintained museums in spite of all the inconveniences they are capable of, certainly served as a hiding place from the wrath of the world old Sun. Where else can one find a cooler place when the whole world outside radiates heat?

Thanks are owed to the unbearable *khatri veyil* and the mind-boggling loneliness, both of which are capable of driving anyone to the edge of madness. But for these two reasons I would not have ventured into the Pondicherry museum, whose incumbents mostly preserved in showcases, are bound to uninterest me like any dull subject, say, algebra or trigonometry.

I never knew that I would be lonely inside the museum too. I found the curator sleeping in his chair with his short and sturdy legs resting criss-cross on the table in front, with a few registers piled up on it.

My presence did not disturb him, though it pulled an elderly lady on the verge of retirement out from a nearby room. She simply raised her eyebrows at me, perhaps signalling me to answer her unasked question about the purpose of my visit.

"I would like to see the museum," I said, "Where should I buy the entrance ticket from?"

"There is no such thing here. Simply enter your name and address in the register on that table and go anywhere you like. We close at six sharp in the evening. And don't get lost," said the lady.

"You mean you'll lock me in if I don't get out in time?"

"Of course…you can't expect me to go from room to room and drive out our visitors. By 5.50 we ring a bell which is only an indication that you should quit the museum. And museum, as you know, is not a good place to spend the night."

I shrugged my shoulders in sheer fear for I believe in ghosts and I am sure museums are the best haunting places for ghosts and ghouls.

"You don't expect visitors at this hour?" I asked.

"This is no tourist season. Museums are no locals' paradise. Perhaps you are the first and last visitor for this afternoon session," said the lady and disappeared into the room wherefrom she emerged.

While I wrote my name in the entry register, the curator half-opened his eyes and looked at me in a daze. He then quickly closed his eyes and rushed back to his dreamland.

The first room displayed weapons of warfare that in any other museum would have remained untouchables. But here they were lying on the floor with a cautionary placard announcing 'Do not step on these'.

It is, of course, risky to step on them for many of them for want of proper care have rusted, and if we stump our toes on them, we are sure to die of tetanus.

My eyes rowed from one weapon to the other till they stood riveted to a sword and a shield. They looked similar to the ones I saw in Trivandrum. And to compare notes would be futile for there are people who safeguard our heritage and there are people who consider that as a big bother.

Somebody's minus is somebody else's plus. I felt an instant urge to hold the sword in one hand and the shield in the other and sincerely hoped that their very presence in my hands would make me a warrior and catapult me to a bygone era.

I bent down to pick up the sword first. Desiring to swish it in different directions, I grasped at its hilt. But it was so sturdy and heavy that it refused to budge. I then pressed both my hands into action. The sword showed signs of yielding to my temptation.

Huff…huff…puff…huff…yeah! I was lifting the sword… I was lifting the sword…but to what extent? I managed it up to my knee and that too with great difficulty. Then I gave up, My back began to ache. I could not hold it further and the sword was back to its place. Great hopes! What a fool am I to lift the sword over my head?

I learnt my lessons from the sword. The shield, as big as the shell of giant tortoise, really scared the shit out of me. Oh, God! Had I tried with it first, things would have become different. With dislocated shoulder joints I would be resting in a hospital.

That set the ball rolling. I can't even lift the sword. And to heave the shield is out of question. But how did my ancestors in Pondicherry manage this sort of acrobatics? My God! What sort of giants were they? The very idea of their strength kept me flabbergasted for long till I entered the next room exhibiting the vehicles used by the French and the Indians in Pondicherry a century or two ago.

That big and palatial hall was cooler and so heart-warming. I felt like sitting in one of the vehicles and enjoy a siesta.

I moved from a *thookku* to a *pallakku,* very much in use among the moneyed people of Pondicherry and then to a huge palanquin. I was all the time wondering what great beauties would have travelled in such vehicles and what sturdy musclemen would have prided themselves on carrying them on their rocking shoulders.

Next to the huge palanquin stood a real eye-catcher. It was a vehicle with three wheels – two big ones at the back supporting a single seater and a small one in the front with a steering rod attached to it. Its long handle protruded backwards to the seat so that the occupier could direct the movement of the vehicle and handle it with ease.

At first, I wondered if it was a cart pulled by animals. But there was no sign of yoke. Then I thought of it differently. But I found no pedal or chain anywhere in the vehicle. My thoughts went weird. And I could not arrive at any decision about the vehicle. But the urge to sit in it began to overwhelm me. I touched the seat. It was made of wood, very solid and strong. Using both the hands I shook the vehicle to know how rickety it has become. Age did not wither it.

I climbed on to it and sat snugly on the wooden seat and held the long steering rod in my right hand and turned it to the left. The front wheel turned to its left with a screech.

"Who is it?" came a gruff voice.

I was about to jump out of the vehicle for fear that I would be fined for not following the rules of the museum.

But before I could do that, a lean man of medium build stood in front of me from nowhere.

His appearance and his apparel looked quite strange to me, for the like of him I had seen only in Pondicherry government calendars. He sported a fully-grown moustache as black as the black dye, both sides twirled up and the stubble on his cheeks and chin told me that he had not shaven for the last few days. He had a lush growth of hair on his head all cleanly oiled and combed and rolled into a bun and looked like a broken horn on the left side of his head. He was hairy all over his body. A dhoti as white as healthy teeth worn differently like a loin-cloth exposed his sturdy thighs and legs. He had a sash that ran across his torso like a broad belt. But it rarely covered his hairy chest and back. Both his wrists had bracelets made of silver. He wore silver anklets studded with rubies.

He looked at me as if I were from another world. The stranger really gave a jolt to my sleep that was trying to hug me. Petrified I asked him, "Who are you?"

"Don't repeat me.... Answer me," came the curt reply.

"I...I...I am a visitor." My voice shivered.

"How dare you sit in this pousse-pousse used by Monsieur Pierre?"

"Pousse-pousse?"

"Yes! In French it is pousse-pousse and in English it means 'push-push'." He replied.

I found an answer to my tormenting question. So, the vehicle was pushed from behind and the man who took the seat steered its direction, applied break when necessary and so on and so forth. My face brightened up.

"And who is Monsieur Pierre?" I asked without any hesitation.

"He was a secretary to the French government in Pondicherry. He used this pousse-pousse till he breathed his last," said the unidentified man.

"And who are you?" I asked.

"A blacksmith who gave life to the dreamy design of Monsieur Pierre," he said with pride-filled face. He then attracted my attention to the golden ear studs that adorned his earlobes and said, "Monsieur Pierre awarded me with these…a magnanimous Frenchman."

My curiosity-filled eyes perhaps probed into his past.

"This fellow for whom I made this pousse-pousse was a woman-eater," he began with a wink. He heaved a sigh, God knows for what reason, and then continued: "He liked the local brown beauties and they too liked him for his white skin."

"He was not married perhaps?" I interrupted, my cultural doubt having raised its head.

"Well! Of course he was married. His wife was a real beauty. I saw her only once when he invited me home to show me his pencil sketch of a vehicle he had drawn out of his imagination and asked me to design it with iron and wood," he replied.

"Why then did he take a liking for local brown beauties? Perhaps his wife was not tasty?" I reciprocated with a wink.

"Don't betray your poor knowledge about the French," he reprimanded me and added, "Frenchmen are real gluttons when it comes to wine, women and food. Their women too had their own clandestine ways. It was this white people's insatiable lust for the warmth of human bodies that had created Creoles in Pondicherry."

I stood spell-bound. He continued. "This vehicle was made to order. When I was giving final touches to this vehicle, Pierre came to my smithy and said, 'You have created a palanquin on wheels. You may get many more such orders. Some intelligent fellow will one day improve upon my design and advise you to make a beautifully improved version of my pousse-pousse'."

"The vehicle was pushed from behind?" I wanted to confirm.

"Of course! That is why it is named pousse-pousse. The man behind would push the vehicle forward, then gather speed and run pushing it as fast as he could shouting at intervals ' pousse-pousse, pousse-pousse', thereby warning the people on the path to move aside," he said daubing the hem of his sash against his face.

"Coming to the most interesting part of the story," he said showing all his teeth that have gone brown owing to intensive pan chewing, "Pierre had fear of the public opinion and feared his wife too. I was told he had a shrew for his wife. Yet he never resisted the temptation of visiting his beloved brownies. And that is why Pierre designed his own vehicle so as not to get noticed in public."

"He could have very well used a palanquin that was in vogue during his days in Pondicherry," I said to show off my knowledge of local history.

"Don't be stupid," he reprimanded, "Pierre was no nitwit. The Government higher-ups on official trips used palanquins. The other palanquin users were mostly women. And so Pierre wanted a vehicle for himself."

"He could have been easily identified," I said to snub the blacksmith.

"I told you that Pierre was not as stupid as you are. He lived at a time when street lamps were not even heard of. People rarely stirred out of their houses after the sunset; and, on unavoidable circumstances, they carried a hurricane lamp in hand to save themselves from the ditches on their path. And Pierre chose the nights to visit his mistresses."

"Quite interesting!" I said in all jubilance.

"I'll tell you something more interesting," said he.

I looked at him like a child with my mouth wide agape.

"Pierre moved out of his house under the pretext of going to his office to look into the urgent files. He returned home very late and thereby kept his green-eyed wife away from suspicion. Pierre parked his vehicle in some darker corner amidst bushy trees and allowed his pusher to sit in the pousse-pousse and sleep comfortably till he returned. This way Pierre had his fill arousing no suspicion in his wife," he said laughing most of the time.

I too had my laugh. Amidst my laughter, I asked him, "But why did you choose to tell me your story?"

"Pierre's story," he corrected.

"Yes! Yes! Pierre's story…But why me of all people?"

The blacksmith laughed like a shower of granites unloaded from a tilting truck. His voice faded as he began to vanish.

Gr…r…r…

It was the warning bell. I woke up with a start. I must hurry up before the museum keeper locks me in. I jumped out of the pousse-pousse as I cursed myself for not having asked the final question: "Was not Madame Pierre clever enough to find out her husband's destinations from the pousse-pousse pusher?"

"You are as stupid as ever," came a voice from nowhere. I was sure that it was the blacksmith's.

My physical eyes ran hither and thither in search of him. They couldn't locate him. But my ears heard him perfectly well: "You are as stupid as ever. Pierre put his brain to proper use. The pousse-pousse pusher Monsieur Pierre employed was a blind man."

□

Beardless Days

Behind every beard, there is a story. Blessed are women. Like a hunter in the thick of the forest searching with his vigilant eyes for a beast of prey, I have hunted down successfully many wild stories lurking behind the wilderness of beards. Pepper beard, salt and pepper beard, and salt beard are real delicacies for the storyteller's mind.

Most of the stories I heard from bearded men are sad and weird. The longer the beard, the sadder the story it tells.

This is not to say that only beards can tell stories. Do not be surprised if I tell you the story of a beardless chin. Remember, I said 'beardless' and not 'shaven' chin.

Stories told in first person singular are definitely appealing and I have read and enjoyed several such stories from the pens of master storytellers from several parts of the globe. Only Goddess Saraswathi and her vehicle know whether these stories really happened to those writers. That is not my concern here.

Having said all these in the way of a preamble, let me rush now to tell you the story of a beardless chin.

I was seventeen when I finished school and joined the Government Arts College to study further. I gained admission to a Pre-University class, which, in turn, would fetch me a seat in a degree course of my choice after a year.

I was poor in mathematics. Not a day passed in school without my being graced by the cane of a dhoti and bush-coat clad teacher who found delight in seeing youngsters wriggle in pain. Since I scored above average marks in the school final exam – God does miracles – I was asked to go to the first of the three groups, meant for the pre-university class students.

The first group offered Mathematics, Physics and Chemistry for main subjects. Since the course was offered to me without my asking for it, I happily and readily joined. The joy did not last longer than expected. It was all due to the compulsion created by the higher-ups who believed that extra-curricular activities were necessary for beginners.

After a week or so, a senior student from the Naval Wing read out a list of the proposed candidates for naval force.

I became quite jubilant. I had a fascination for pure white clothes and the Naval Wing had only white uniforms. Beret, socks, shoes were also in white…

"Enjoy the pleasure of riding the seas," I said to myself. I was already sailing an imaginary ship. And when I anchored the ship and reached the land of reality, I found that one more item was waiting for my benefit. That was swimming.

I was an adept at swimming inside a broad well in my village. In fact, it was the place where my playmates taught me the art of swimming. I swam with fish and non-poisonous water snakes. But I never tried this art in a lake near my house for fear that the woodcutters and farmers working in the woods and fields would report the matter to my father, who, with a wag of his finger, cautioned me almost everyday. Now I would swim in the seven seas and to the delight of my father, I would get a certificate at the end of the course.

I was really overwhelmed by the benefits listed out by the senior… *boori Kizhangu* and tea at the end of the parade everyday and the amount that would be given as washing allowance at the end of the week were real attractions.

"Above all, you are trained to guard the Nation's seas and oceans," said the senior before he left. That was the only point that went over my head.

That did not matter.

The next day the enlisted 'sailors' were asked to fall in a single file. Height, weight, chest measurements, this test and that test... wow! I was selected. My dreams became colourful.

Two days later, we were given uniforms with the strict instruction that, before we are on parade, we should stand before the life-size mirror and ask ourselves, "Am I Smart?"

I was Smart. My father appreciated my courage. But my mother began to shed tears for fear of losing me to the Nation and the ocean.

"Hei! Shut up! By joining the Naval Wing, this fellow is not going to be sent on a warship to fight battles and conquer countries. This is part of the game the Institution plays... You don't have to feel for this." My father consoled my mother.

My mother was not ready to believe him in this matter, though she believed him in toto in all other matters.

My father and I kept quiet knowing that she would not stop shedding tears till she decided to do so.

Minutes later she dried her eyes and cheeks with the hem of her sari, inhaled the air a bit noisily and said, "Whatever is destined will happen."

"Good! It all happens for the good," concluded my father.

The date and time were fixed for the first parade. That was three days away. I was on cloud nine. In my over-enthusiasm, I looked out for a senior and asked him, "Excuse me, Sir! The first parade will take place on land or on sea?"

The senior sneered at me. I was confused. I tried my doubt with a couple of other seniors. One went away laughing behind his sleeves. But the other answered with a sardonic grin: "Oh! You don't know? The first parade will take place inside the sea."

"Sir! My knowledge of the Naval Wing is next to nothing. Please tell me what I should understand by your words, 'inside the sea'?" I pleaded with the senior.

"Inside the sea! Oh! You don't know. Now listen, 'inside the sea' means 'inside the sea'," replied the senior in all humility.

"You mean in the depth of the sea, Sir!" I asked with a stupid grin on my face.

"Yes! That's right," he said and moved away from my sight.

As soon as I reached home after college, I put on the uniform, stood before the mirror, asked myself 'Are you Smart?' and got the answer, "Yes! You are smart." I posed before my mother who started admiring my looks. Before I changed to my usual lungi and sleeveless banian, I saluted my image in the mirror. In fact, I was proud of myself.

The first parade, to my disappointment, took place on an untidy and unkempt ground inside the college campus.

Before the start of the drill, the Lieutenant in command scrutinized every one of us, as if he were doing it under a microscope. He was satisfied with our appearance. Then he gave a short talk in his stentorian voice: "Our next parade will be fifteen days hence. It will take place on our seashore behind the statue of Mahatma Gandhi. Black leather shoes for the land parade and white canvas shoes for the sea."

His talk made me happy beyond words and the word 'sea' took me to dizzy heights.

"I repeat," continued the Lieutenant, "the next parade will happen after the fifteenth day. You are given such a long time because you should sport an anchor beard, along with your well-trimmed drooping moustaches. If you can't grow a beard within this period, then come to the parade with a clean-shaven face… No beard…Then no moustache."

His last few words came like a bolt from the blue.

I sported a fine moustache like my father. But I was not sure of my beard. I took a close look at my chin with the help of a mirror and I could count the hairs there. And each hair seemed to be estranged from the other. What should I do?

My hunt for advice began. Some suggested that I should apply coconut oil to my cheeks and chin. This I should do quite often and see that my face is continuously oily. A little bottle of coconut oil became my constant companion.

A friend of mine who already had a thick growth of hair on his chin and cheeks advised me to shave myself daily. I shaved myself twice a day. Thanks to my father's razors.

Thirteen days rolled by. But for several cuts and bruises all over my face, nothing miraculous happened. My disappointment was beyond words.

Since I could find no picture of any Hindu God sporting a beard, I prayed before a picture of Jesus Christ, himself praying on a mountain. Oh, what a fine beard he had! If only I could grow such a beard, I would certainly command respect. Looks matter very much. But my prayers didn't yield any fruit.

The day fixed for the second parade on the seashore came. But no new hair came up in my face. "No beard… no moustache." the Lieutenant's words kept reverberating in my ears.

I had no other go but shave off my lovely moustache. The mirror said: "You look horrible." I turned my face away from the view of the mirror. I was in tears.

I searched for my mother for a second opinion. I found her in the backyard of the house, sweeping aside the dead leaves in our little garden.

Hiding my upper lip with the palm of my right hand, I stood before her. She was engrossed in her work.

"Amma!" I attracted her attention, and said, "Tell me frankly about my looks now."

I lowered my hand with a jerk. My upper lip came into full view.

My mother, as if shocked to the core, raved. "You brat! What have you done to your moustache?" Then in a fit of fury, she began to thrash me all over with the broom she had in her hand, all the time howling. "Will you do it ever again? Will you do it ever again?"

I was trying to dodge her blows but she was such an adept at wielding the broom that I couldn't escape any of them. I ran from tree to tree, but she chased me like a hound and continued with her thrashings and howling.

My father, sensing danger, came rushing to the spot.

"Stop it..." he howled at my mother. "How dare you do this to a grown-up boy?"

My mother threw the broom to one corner of the garden, and said pointing her finger to my upper lip, "Look at what he has done... He has killed you."

I was taken aback.

My father came nearer to me. He looked daggers at me and then slapped me twice on both my cheeks, and then gave a punch to my chin.

"Never again do this to your face, till I die; we are *Kshatriyas,*" my father said and left the scene.

My dream of the ocean and the Nation shattered, I stood deep-rooted to the earth. My tear glands swelled but no tear trickled out.

□

A Day in the Life of a Coolie

A Day in the life of a Coolie.

That was the line my cell phone screen displayed when I clicked the button to read the SMS. The message was sent by my boss who had great faith in me and in my work. He was not that type of boss who would assign work only to his 'working reporters' and clear cheques to his 'sleeping reporters'. He made every one of us sweat for our food, though he never grudged paying us handsomely. None of us for our part ever had any complaint against him.

My boss always loved to assign challenging topics to me and I too loved to take them up. From teaching school kids, I switched over to an electronic two-wheeler agency and after a period of four months as its assistant sales manager, I crossed floors and moved on to work as the sales manager of a motor car company that sold used cars. There was nothing challenging in those jobs that brought me food and shelter. And when I took up the job of a reporter for a daily eveninger called 'Buzzing Bee', I found my life worth living.

My duty was to report any untoward incident anywhere I was roaming, interview people of the lower strata of society, write reviews of new films of my choice and also take up any special assignment my boss specified.

Such special assignments were always meant for the Sunday Magazine section of the newspaper, and my boss was meticulous in selecting not only the topic for the cover story but also the right man for doing that job.

I was happy that my boss's choice fell on me for writing the cover story for the week.

It was customary of my boss to SMS the title of the story on Friday night. He wanted the cover story at the proof-read stage and the relevant photographs on Sunday positively by 10 in the morning on his desk.

To write about a day in the life of a coolie...huh! It is not as easy as writing a paper for a stupid Seminar. If the academician can command two buttons in the keyboard – cut and paste – then the scholarly paper would be just a clicking distance away. But my job demanded field study and I had to run after someone without being noticed. That sent me on a long inner journey into unknown parts. For hours I had followed false trials, ending in blind alleys, and only lately I managed to find the road that should lead me to my journey's end.

By the time I finished doing my homework, it was midnight. And for a reporter like me, midnight would be too early to go to bed unless newly married. But I had to on that night for my next day was expected to begin too early for me.

I set the alarm clock in my cell phone. For your information, I do not even wear a wrist watch for my cell phone was everything to me. And sleep hugged me.

Saturday: 4.30 a.m.

The alarm did startle me and I woke up. I was fresher than before, and immediately warmed up to my job.

5.30 a.m.

I have already reached the chosen slum. Poor coolies hail from such places. I could see the Sun struggling to get up, but I was surprised to see the slum already active. Silhouettes sweeping the little front-yard clean, silhouettes sprinkling water, silhouettes drawing kolams, silhouettes carrying plastic pitchers in both their hands and rushing towards the only street tap, silhouettes carrying pitchers filled with water in each hand, and balancing a plastic kudam brimming with water on their head.

It was a feast for my eyes to see silhouettes of women doing this and silhouettes of women doing that. My mind began to carry me to dizzy heights, as the French saying flashed across my mind: "All women are fair when all the candles are out."

I pulled out a cigarette from a plastic case, tucked it in between my lips and lit it.

I took in a deep whiff of smoke and a few seconds later pushed the smoke out through my nostrils like the Chinese dragon.

"Hei! Who's that? There are only huts and huts here. Are you blind? By the way who the hell are you?" A silhouette howled.

"I am a reporter," I replied.

"What? A porter?...But I am sure you do not belong to this slum…Are you searching for someone?" The silhouette came nearer.

"I told you I am a reporter. And that means I write for the newspaper," I said walking towards the moving silhouette.

"Oh, you mean you are a newspaper man!" she exclaimed. "Are you going to write about us?"

"Of course! I am in search of a coolie and I will be writing about his life today," I said showing all my teeth to her for that would be the only visible thing in my body at that hour.

"You take us for landlords or what? All of us are coolies here. Why don't you write about me?" she asked in an eager tone.

"Huh! Enough of women. Too many stories have been written about women in our newspapers. I would like to write about a male coolie," I said coolly.

"It seems you are fed up with women," she commented and continued: "You people who make a living with a pen find your pockets full of women. What can you poor creatures do, when women run after you! We have a poet in our slum. He composes and sings songs and sometimes we hear his songs repeated in films. He gets some money but the women here fleece him."

"A lyricist in the slum! That sounds interesting," I said to myself. "Where does he live?" I asked.

She smiled and said, "We are standing just in front of his hut."

I was shocked to the marrow. "In this ramshackle hut lives a lyricist? Oh, who can ever understand the vagaries of Fate?"

"Oh, no! You don't have to talk about Fate and all. He was born here and so he loves this place. His wife hanged herself long ago giving him his freedom to choose his life. He is quite a happy guy and makes many women here happy," she said softly. "His name is Bhagawan and he is real Bhagawan," she added.

6:00 a.m.

At last, day broke and I looked about. A little more than thirty huts budded into view. I could still see women very active outside their huts, some drying their washed linen, some banging their linen against a stone slab near the water tap and some driving away the dirt from their linen with a soap cake.

Bhagawan came out of his hut. He has kilted up his multi-coloured lungi and his shorts were peeping out. He had covered his torso with a blue T-shirt; a white towel that passed for his headgear. He locked the door of his hut, pushed the key into his shorts pocket, slipped his feet into a pair of flip-flop and began to march without taking notice of me.

"That's good. Let me follow him without being noticed," I said to myself and literally ran after him to cope with his speed.

6.30 a.m.

Bhagawan slowed down as he neared a teashop. "Bhagawan...Bhagawan...Bhagawan is coming." I heard many people in the teashop murmur. Those who were sipping tea stood up and greeted him by raising their paper teacups above their heads. Those who were waiting for their supply of tea simply stood up and bowed in respect. And those who could not find seats in the teashop and waiting for their turn moved closer to Bhagawan to shake hands with him. But Bhagawan smiled and waved his right hand to all the people in all directions.

The tea master came rushing towards him with a glass of steaming hot tea. Bhagawan bowed before him and took the glass in his right hand. He then moved out of the teashop to the open ground and raised his glass towards the Heavens before he took his first sip. He paused before he took a second sip and then putting the edge of the glass to his lips...gluck...gluck...gluck. Placing the empty glass on a mound of sand, he pulled out a bidi from the upper end of his left ear and stuck it between his lips.

Someone in the crowd of tea drinkers came running towards him with a matchbox in hand. Bhagawan smiled at him and with a wag of his right accusing finger warned him not to give any help unless asked for.

I saw Bhagawan smoking. But no puff of smoke ever came out of his mouth or nostrils...not even from his ears or eyes. On a keen watch I discovered that he was gulping down every puff of smoke. He made the best use of his bidi and when it was about to burn his lips, he spat out the stub.

Bhagawan bent down to pick up the tea glass, moved inside and paid for the tea. He began to walk faster than before.

7:00 a.m.

"This is what we call Bhagawan time. Our clocks may fail to show the right time. But when Bhagawan enters the harbour, it is exactly 7 o'clock in the morning," I heard one in the crowd of coolies say so.

Bhagawan sporting a gleeful face entered the harbour. He waved his hands in all directions showing all his teeth that were perfectly white.

A brown man, perhaps a port officer, clad in white dhoti and shirt made his appearance in the harbour and there was absolute silence. He then beckoned Bhagawan. Bhagawan too moved out of the crowd and bowed in all humility before the brown man.

"Well done, Bhagawan. Well done...I spent a lot of time in listening to your hits yesterday night at home. There was no power supply for more than four hours in my place and my little transistor relieved me of boredom. Everybody likes your melodies," the brown man appreciated.

As Bhagawan made no reply, the brown man said, "You might at least answer when you're spoken to."

Bhagawan shot a little glance sideways at the brown man. He then turned away with a rueful smile.

"That's Bhagawan," said the brown man and looked interested. "You are a happy sort of person, aren't you? God, I'd like to be you."

Bhagawan nodded as he began to hum, at first under his breath, then louder: "She was my woman and she did me wrong..."

The brown man hummed the same song to himself and said, "Well then! All of you sign in the register and go to work."

7:45 a.m.

About a hundred or so coolies stood in a much disciplined queue and moved into a small room. Soon the queue disappeared. Perhaps there was another exit into the harbour. I felt flustered. I emboldened myself to walk into the small room in spite of the warning board at the entrance that said 'Prohibited Area. Trespassers will find their watery grave'.

Once inside the small room, the brown man welcomed me with all smiles. Perhaps he was carried away by a still camera hanging from my neck, and a little voice-recorder in my hand. He cleared his throat and combed his hair with his fingers. He then tidied himself up before he asked me to occupy a chair in front of his seat.

Something in me told me that I should hurry up with my mission before he misunderstood me. And I didn't waste time. He listened to me with rapt attention. He threw back his head and laughed – a shrill laugh without merriment. "Do tell me what you make of Bhagawan? We're all so excited about him," he said slowly.

There was a pause. Then the brown man said doubtfully: "But I should hardly think it possible that a man would do that – to his wife. You know his marriage to an actress was the greatest surprise. She was supposed to be going to marry a film director and then suddenly she gets engaged to this man no one had ever heard of!"

"You know her well, Sir?" I said with a slight mock-modest laugh. The brown man shot a quick glance at me and said: "No, but a sister-in-law of mine is one of her best friends." He was silent a moment and then went on, "That young actress was very much in the news and she knows how to advertise herself all right."

"But, Sir! I am here to write about a day in the life of a coolie. But you are dragging me into Bhagawan's history," I tried to change the subject.

"You call yourself a reporter, eh!" the brown man ejaculated. "I am just trying to remember you what really happened one day in Bhagawan's life."

I shrugged my shoulders. I thought to myself: "I bet he has something interesting to tell me."

Now that the story was taking a different turn, I looked thoughtfully at him. He gave a chortle of pure delight when he realised he had won. "I have seen every kind of fool in my life. Only one kind is difficult to understand." He was silent a minute and then repeated in a slightly different tone of voice: "Yes, only one kind – the fool in love." He gave a vexed laugh. I joined his laughter.

The brown man went on: "I simply report to you what my sister-in-law told me long ago. I do not even remember the names of the director and the actress. Alzheimer has already walked into my mind. I vaguely remember the day the actress got married to our Bhagawan. It was unexpected and the marriage took place in the Registrar's office. No invitation and no dinner to anyone. Newspaper reporters are clever people and they made the news very sensational, highlighting the actress's love with the film director. Every newspaper invented its own reason as to why the actress had walked out on the director. No newspapers ever mentioned the name Bhagawan but insulted him by calling him a coolie. Of course, he was a coolie but he liked and respected his job. He prided himself by saying that a beautiful and well-to-do-woman had married a coolie. That meant love spells death to ego. And Bhagawan was a human being to the core."

I sighed and said, "I never know how people manage to do that." The brown man said in a philosophical tone, "How will you know what it is to get burnt on the funeral pyre unless you die? I know. This love business gets hold of you and you can't do anything about it. Let me go to Bhagawan's story. It happened four years ago, maybe, I am not sure. Bhagawan and his team were doing overtime here in this harbour unloading goods from a huge ship and they worked continuously for twenty-four hours without a break. By eight in the morning, Bhagawan got his payment and left for his home only to find his wife hanging from a bamboo ceiling of his hut."

"Why? What happened?" I was curious to know.

"I don't know," said the brown man in a low tone. "Nobody knows about it for that matter. It was rumoured that the director had sent his henchmen to finish her off. It was also rumoured that she did it when she was convinced that it was all her fault. But nobody said a word against our Bhagawan. I would say Bhagawan should not have allowed her to die when she chose him as her life-partner. From that day, Bhagawan stopped speaking to others. In the morning, he takes a glass of hot tea and a bidi. Well, that is his food till he goes back home to cook his dinner. People tell me that he does not let out the smoke. Perhaps he feels that his stomach should burn all through the day. Is it to keep himself active to avenge the death of his wife? Only Bhagawan knows." He finished the tale by raising his hands heavenward.

10:00 p.m.

Back in my room, I flung myself on my sofa-cum-bed. It's time to start tapping at my laptop. The deadline is quite near. The topic 'A Day in the Life of a Coolie' began to haunt me.

□

The Prismatic Pain

Stunned stood Sundaram.

For a minute or so, his healthy eyes saw nothing but vacuum. His mind was a complete blank.

What pushed him to such a regretful situation was an unwarranted act of his father, Ramadurai. Like everybody else, Sundaram treated his father as his hero and worshipped him in his heart of hearts. To make it short, he was a role model for the young man.

An aimless life is a useless life… Sundaram had heard his father say so oft and on. He used to repeat it to his friends, explicate it with the examples passed on by his father and spoke at length of his own aim in life. He also narrated to his friends all that his father had said about the way of the world and the right path to be chosen for a better way of living.

He distinctly remembered his father's words on the importance of the body and the proper way of maintaining it.

"Listen, Sunda! God has blessed us with a body and no part of it can be discarded. He has measured everything both inside and outside and put them all in their proper places. If you lose any chunk of your body, then you become a cripple for life. Therein lies the greatness of the creator." Ramadurai paused raising both his hands towards the Heavens, with a sense of seriousness on his face.

Sundaram looked intently at his father and asked in a mischievous tone, "But you rush me to the barber's shop once in three weeks and every Sunday after bath you 'cut' my nails."

Ramadurai was unable to control his laughter.

"Why do you laugh, father? Aren't hair and nails part of our body?"

"True, my boy! But they grow. They grow even after we die," replied Ramadurai.

"Oh, is that why people offer their hair to the gods in the temple?" Sundaram mumbled. A steely glint began to shine in his eyes.

"They can't afford to offer their head or thumb, though there are tall tales about the offering of such parts to the Divine." Ramadurai made a snide remark.

"But you don't allow me to grow long hair or sharp nails, like many of the heroes I come across in comics and movies." Sundaram poured out his heart.

"I told you, Sunda, all that grows have to be cut… Don't we cut our rose plants in our terrace garden to size, so that there will be fine buds and blooms?" said Ramadurai with exemplary self-assurance.

Sundaram smiled tremulously. He looked at his father from the corners of his eyes and said, "But father, you said, our brain too grows." A mischievous smile began to occupy his face.

"It has to…my boy," replied Ramadurai in a measured voice. "If it does not grow, we will then pass for idiots. But this growth is different from the one we are talking about."

Sundaram wrinkled up his eyebrows. Ramadurai understood that his son needed a short lecture.

"Every one of us is endowed with a brain that weighs equally with the others. That is what we call physical growth. But there is another growth called mental growth. This refers to the quality of the brain."

Sundaram shook his head either way and betrayed his ignorance. His father came to realise that his son needed further explanation. He was after all a boy and these things might go over his head, unless explained properly by a proper person.

"Now listen, Sunda! If I throw a volley-ball at you, how do you catch it?"

Sundaram, who was listening with a lot of interest, answered immediately, "With both my hands, father."

"Good! And if I give a toffee to you?" His voice was a musical drag.

"I will receive it with my cupped hand." Sundaram said with a sense of joy.

"Very good! If I give you one end of a piece of thread?"

"Ah! With the forefinger and thumb," pat came the answer.

"Excellent, my boy. That shows the growth of your brain. Had I asked you such questions a couple of years before, you would have given me only wrong answers."

"Wrong answers! What do you say, Father! How do you know that I would have given you wrong answers?"

"I know… because you were too young for such questions."

"Young may be… but not too young for your questions. Perhaps your father thought so when you were young and so did not ask you such questions. But we kids these days are different from the run-of-the-mill children. And so, father, don't ever underestimate my worth."

Ramadurai was bamboozled by such an answer. It was rather unexpected. He took time to respond. But he did it differently: "You see, how your brain has developed! Ha… Ha…Ha…" He added after a pause, "I am proud of you, my son. You are really a precocious child."

Sundaram had such a fine relationship with his father. Ramadurai was everything to Sundaram. He adored him in all possible ways and sometimes called him his god. Ramadurai too treated Sundaram as a friend. In addition, he was philosopher and guide to the young man.

No wonder that Sundaram was shocked to see his father indulge in such an unexpected action, unwarranted of him.

"What have you done? What have you done?" screamed Sundaram at his father, as he came out of his daze.

Ramadurai looked at his son. Sundaram was standing with his eyes closed and his body was trembling. Was he on the verge of shedding tears? He moved towards his son. He then bent down and looked intently at him. "Are you scared, my son?" He asked.

Sundaram nodded his head. His eyes were fear filled.

Ramadurai lifted his son a little up, hugged him and then pressed his head against his hairy chest. But Sundaram released himself quickly and looked daggers at his father.

"Why do you look at me like that?" Ramadurai asked.

"You say one thing and do another," the boy said. "You used to say every part of our body is essential and that they have to remain intact. If a man loses even his pinky, then he is no more a complete man."

"True! I do not go back on my words, my boy. Pinky or thumb… they should be intact. Let me tell you something more. One can still breathe even if one's nose is cut off. One can still hear even if one's ears are lopped off. But you can imagine how ugly one would look without nose and ears. In god's creation, everything was put in its proper place. You lose a part, you lose your shape. Every shape is divinely." Ramadurai declared with an amiable smile.

"Hm…ah…Going by that logic, the scorpion too needs its tail. Why did you cut off its tail with the scissors you use for trimming your moustaches?" Sunda's voice emitted fire.

Ramadurai felt that he was trapped. A wave of guilt rose in him and he fumbled for words. "Oh, sonny! You do not know how poisonous that scorpion is! It deserves only such a treatment for entering our home."

"You could have very well crushed it to death. Everything would have been over with that poisonous animal by this time. But what did you do to that poor creature? You have maimed its tail."

"Not its tail… only its sting," corrected the father.

"It all means the same, father! I remember a story you once told me of a sage taking his morning bath in a pond when he saw a scorpion that accidentally fell in water, struggling for its life. The sage took pity on the insect, and allowed it to climb onto his palm. The next moment the scorpion with a swish of its tail stung the palm of the sage. He shook his hand vigorously in pain and the creature once again landed on water and struggled for its life. The good-hearted sage took pity on it again and tried to help by allowing it to climb on to his accusing finger. The scorpion reached for the finger and again stung him. Writhing in pain, the sage understood that it was its nature to sting. And after all, what is the sting for? When you finished the story, my dear pa, you said "What are scorpions without their stings? What are snakes without their fangs?"

Ramadurai dropped languidly onto the couch. He kept his arms folded against his chest, his legs crossed and his right leg swinging resolutely.

"I cut off the sting because I didn't want to kill the scorpion," Ramadurai said.

"You could have very well killed it, father. Now the scorpion may not have second thoughts in becoming food for the hen at the backyard."

A mild tremor seemed to roll down Ramadurai's body. He began to swing his leg even more resolutely. Seconds later, he sprang from the couch and searched for the scorpion on the wall.

"What if the sting is gone! It will grow again," he said casually without looking at the face of his son.

"No. You lie. You once told me that only geckos are blessed with new tail, once they lose theirs in accidents and that no scorpion would ever be blessed with a sting once again," retorted Sundaram.

Amazed at the memory of his son, Ramadurai smiled to himself and continued his search for the scorpion.

The scorpion was found moving in a circle, perhaps searching for its lost sting.

Stealthily, Ramadurai approached the wall. His movement slowed to an indolent glide. He took the scorpion by its tail and dangled it before his son. "Now you see! The deadly scorpion is a harmless creature." He punctuated his bravado with a reckless cackle.

"But father, what are we without our limbs? For a scorpion, its tail is a very important limb. It is nothing without it. And you too would not have dared to touch it. I know you are not as foolish as the sage in your story."

Ramadurai moaned and threw the helpless scorpion to the floor.

Sundaram picked it up by its tail and rushed to the backyard of the house.

When he came back into the house, his father saw a smile lingering on his face. "What have you done to the scorpion?" Ramadurai asked, glancing furtively over his glasses in his son's direction.

"What you failed to do," Sundaram whispered with the weak jubilation of a warrior who returns from the field with the head of the enemy somehow in his own hands.

Both father and son heard the hen at the backyard cackle… A cock crowed.

□

Call Yourself a Plant!

Call yourself a plant? Then you should flower.

No matter what colour or shape is your flower! It matters little even if it emanates foul odour. You should by all means flower.

Every plant should bloom. A flower is a flower even if there is nothing in it.

A flower is all that the seven seas, the seven mountains and the seven worlds expect of a plant. Why should you be an exception to it?

There are houses to my left; houses to my right; houses to my face and houses to my back. All these houses have their own garden – plants in the front-yard; plants in the backyard and plants on the terrace.

Oh, what a lovely sight these plants make!

We can feast our eyes upon them. But what a pathetic sight you plants in my gardens make!

You plants in my front-yard! You plants in my backyard! You plants on my terrace! And you special plants inside my house, cool and comfortable! But not a bud, not a bloom do I see anywhere in my gardens. Only plants and plants and plants. Nauseating. Green and green and green everywhere. Pooh! What a sickening sight!

It is the flower that makes the difference. It is the flower that tells the world how productive is the plant. But you plants in my campus seem to be happily unaware of it, eh?

Tell me what I have not done for you? Haven't I watered you everyday? Have I ever skipped a single day? Leave alone rainy days. And for your sake, I forego visiting even my dear ones staying abroad.

Look! You fellows know how much I care for you. I feed you with the best of plant food available from horticulture stores. I see to it that you are not in bad company. Yes! I do not like weeds staring me in the face. I pull out the ageing leaves before they could turn brown and fall off. Huh! I prune you. I do this and I do that. I do this and that, that and this, all for you plants' sake.

But you heartless mercenaries! Ungrateful men! Why are you so indifferent to me? Why are you hiding your flowers when I have performed my duty?

I wish for a flower…only one flower at least. I wonder why even that only one is denied to me.

I am not greedy or overambitious. I don't expect you plants to bear flowers all over, though that would definitely make a lovely sight. Oh! How I would brag and boast of that flower! But why…why not evenone?

What curse has fallen on my garden? What mentally sick woman has cursed me?

I feel like lying on my belly and beat my feet in the sand. This longing is turning into an ache.

Do I pass for a stupid woman? It is not for your physical charms I have planted you all in my campus. I dreamt that one day you will all bring to light your hidden beauty. Oh! All my dreams about you pass for dreams and nothing but dreams. Life moves on only when dreams turn into realities. Fizzled out dreams only dart venom-tipped sharp arrows into our craving heart.

Victoria sank bank in her easy chair, pondering the paradox, all the time fiddling with the stray strand of uncoloured hair clamouring for freedom from the coloured mass. Her image in the looking glass was preparing to repeat hers.

□

The Word Processor

It was story time. I had just finished supper, while watching a couple of late night serials. The nights when I used to tell stories to my children were a thing of the past. They are grown-ups now and give me raw materials for my stories. Therefore, I have made it a point to tell stories to my computer, which, in turn, gives me a saleable printout.

That night I switched my computer on and sat facing the monitor. The C.P.U. was at work and after the usual formalities, it said, "Welcome! Thank you for using the infra CD Rom drive." I clicked the WORD icon and waited for a new document to open up. The word processor was ready and the office assistant, a Robot Duck, barged his way on to the screen.

My hands resting on the keyboard, my deft fingers were ready to tap-tap-tap the story to my silent listener.

Thoughts, strange thoughts, come from somewhere from the body. The 'somewhere' continues to remain a mystery to me even after a period of twenty or twenty-two years of my career as a creative writer. Thoughts sometimes crowd in the 'somewhere' and vie with one another for an outlet. On such occasions, I was usually in a quandary. Sometimes plots too recommend for themselves for immediate attention. What to choose from a cascade of plots?

Closing my eyes, I began fishing for the right catch. The C.P.U. let out a burp and the next moment the monitor displayed the screensaver – boogey baby.

"Oh! Ten minutes have passed since I switched on my PC." I cursed myself.

My hand graced the mouse and the little handy thing spelt death to the boogey baby and resurrected the WORD document and the Robot Duck.

No writer worth his salt ever knew or will ever know the vagaries of creative process. Hours would be wasted in simply staring at the white paper or the blank screen. What to write and what to eschew, what plot to choose and what sort of flesh and skin to select to garb the skeleton? Such occasions could be taxing to writers for they have to sit smiling to themselves finding fault with their own inability to put pen to paper or simply tap-tap-tap. That is the time the writer expects Goddess Saraswathi to come to his rescue, or at least an angel or a devil to descend on him. I was no exception. Perhaps another ten minutes had escaped and the boogey baby was back.

When the boogey baby screensaver was installed, I had spent several minutes in watching the boogey baby dance in the nude. Now I looked daggers at the dancing doll.

My hand moved towards the mouse to bring back the WORD document to life.

"Oh, don't! Your hands off, please. Let the sleeping mouse sleep." It was the computer that spoke.

It was for the first time the computer spoke to me without my command. I sat spellbound.

"What do you take me for? An Idiot box? A nincompoop with no brain of my own?" the computer continued. "How long do you want me to wait, all the time staring at your lousy face? You seem to have gone dry. Well! It's time that you recharge your batteries. Wine and women would help. But I know you are a strange case…no bad habits…you seem to be inspired only by the dead and the living writers who found their way to your grand library."

The computer heaved a sigh. Perhaps it wanted me to respond. However, I was like a child listening to his parents.

"Speak man speak! I am talking only to you. Do not take me for a fool or an ass to simply blink at you and take commands from you."

"No. No! You do not seem to understand my problem at all. I am here to tell you a story but I am yet to select a nice one. Till then please wait." I responded.

"I have waited too long. You do not even allow me to watch the boogey baby dance. There was a time when I struggled to cope with the speed of your story-telling, when your imagination ran riot. Now what the hell has happened to you? Why don't you have a puff? Oh, I am sorry! You don't even smoke. I think I will not be wrong if I brand you a misfit. Writers, prolific writers like you smoke, wine, dine and bed with nubile women. Such activities help them to be creative. I always wonder what kind of a fellow you are to avoid such pleasures of life! I have also wondered what genii are working in you when you told me very nice stories."

"Thank you," I said, "Give me just a few more minutes. I will tell you a fine story." I begged.

"My friend! Do not take me for a ride. For a change, let me tell you a story. Are you willing to listen?"

"Why not? Go ahead then. Let me have the pleasure of listening to a machine."

"I will tell you a story on the condition that you will not call it yours and sign your name when you send it to the press."

I glared at the computer. My face turned blacker still. A sense of shame ran down my spine chilling it to the coccyx. "Believe me. Today it was my dilemma in selecting the plot that had delayed my telling you a story. Don't ever think that my imagination will run dry till I breathe my last and I will never claim myself a father to your child. Then go ahead with your story."

The computer he-hawed, cleared its throat and began its narration.

"Long long ago, no one knows how long ago, lived a computer like me in a cosy house of a writer like you. The computer had no brains to call its own. However, the writer thought that the computer was more powerful and highly imaginative than him. One day..." the computer paused.

Then what happened? Go ahead. I am listening," I said ebbing with enthusiasm.

The computer remained silent.

I wondered what had happened to the story-teller. It didn't take time for me to realise that there was a power failure and the screen was blinking with the help of the UPS which can't give life to the infra.

□

Night Mare

Bartruhari banged his head against a nearby stone pillar as a mark of helplessness.

On second thoughts, he asked himself, "Why should I punish myself?"

Seconds later, he mumbled, "These lecherous rats... Huh! They deserve corporal punishment for their lusty act..."

Something in him said, "Who knows? You may be at fault. Who ever knows who is at fault unless one is prepared to probe into the matter?"

He stood still like a statue, in the dark, watching two silhouettes making a beast of two backs. He was sure of the woman's voice. That was his wife's... the right royal queen's. And the man's voice. He was not sure. That was certainly a man in the royal stable.

The stable keeper! The stable keeper's assistant! The stable watch! The stable cleaner! The stable feeder! He was not quite sure. But certainly a man from the royal stable.

"Oh! My mare! My mare! What a wonderful body you have my lovely mare!" Bartruhari heard the man tell the queen, who was naked to the skin.

"My king! My king! I am all yours. Allow your sturdy hands to move over every bit of my territory, which is all yours," Bartruhari heard his queen tell the stableman who was also naked but for his headgear.

Bartruhari's nerves burned as an upshot of his royal blood running very hot. His hand quickly reached for the hilt of his sharp sword. It was the very same sword that had feasted on the blood and flesh of his enemies who obstructed his path of progress. How many heads of warriors it had rolled off their bodies in all these years!

As he was about to draw the sword, something in him said, "Who ever knows who is at fault unless one is prepared to probe into the matter?" He withdrew his hand as if he had touched live coal. He folded his hands against his chest, as if his hands were tied with an invisible rope. He kept his eyes and ears open.

"What if the king sees us now while we make love?" said the stableman in a hushed voice as the tip of his tongue began to slide down to her earlobe.

"Ha! Great! Don't ever make any mention of the king paralysed in his loins," the queen snorted and slapping him familiarly upon his rump, she giggled.

The stableman winced before he began to make his attempts to draw the first of the several breathless cries from her throat.

"Paralysed in the loins!" King Bartruhari expressed his doubt by a gesture of surprise. "I have lost count of beauties in my harem… Must be in thousands. My enemies too envy me and call me a connoisseur of the fair sex. But this queen of mine…Who ever knows who is at fault unless one is prepared to probe into the matter?"

The queen slightly turned her voluptuous body to offer the stableman a full view of those twin ornaments. They were full, rotund, meaty bubbling with youth. They looked like good grenadiers at attention.

They caught Bartruhari's eyes too. "Spiked helmets – spikes standing up like pointed thimbles," the king said in glee as if he were seeing them for the first time. He heaved a sigh.

"Wah! Wah! What are these? Horse horns! Horse horns! A rarity indeed." The stableman whispered. "They make me dizzy," so saying he rested his dizzy head on the soft buxom pillows.

After a moment, he lowered himself to such a position as to be able to plant a solid kiss upon those juicy jugs and mammoth melons, which were so receptive that the queen could not suppress a cry of pleasure at the emotion his tongue provoked as he began an assiduous probing.

As the stableman's eager and brisk hands began to move over the queen's limbs and breasts with natural grace and instinctive fervour, Bartruhari shut his eyes tightly.

Realisation dawned upon him. Thanks to his enquiring mind. In spite of the innumerable beauties in his harem that was under his service for all the twenty-four hours, he was the most inexperienced lover.

A couple of hot tears trickled out of his closed eyes, and soon disappeared into his well-trimmed beard.

"The vast number of minutes that you take every morning to trim your beard…Ho! Ho! Ho! Had you spent half of those minutes with the queen every night in her bed… Ha! Ha! Ha!..."

The voice he heard was shaky as if disguised. It came quite nearby. He allowed his eyes to roam but in the dark, his eyes were powerless. Hence, he wanted his ears to be attentive, that he might recognise the voice.

There was a long silence after those words.

As if to break the frightening silence, there was laughter in the air, a lax, spangled, spiralling laughter. "Is the queen more beautiful than those charming beauties brought home as booty from many conquered lands?"

The voice he heard was quite youthful and vigorous, as if disguised. It too came from quite a nearby quarter. Bartruhari felt a shrinking of his whole body. He felt it would be futile to search for the black cat in a pitch dark alley. He was sure that he was confronting with himself. He had no other go but to stand still and listen to the arguments and counter-arguments of his soul. He smiled so swiftly that he was not even certain it had been a smile.

"Aren't inner chaos secret volcanoes in search of a fissure through which to explode?" Bartruhari reopened his eyes to find his queen lean over the stableman and joyously impaling herself on the man's sensual mast.

"Wah! Wah! Nothing like a ride on a man of one's choice. A hundred or so husbands cannot equal a stallion like you," the queen said in delight.

"I know all the trickeries in this war of love," the stableman's voice was higher and thinner.

"Trickeries in this war of love... Ha! Ha..Ha! How many of these you are familiar with?" The king heard the shaky voice again.

Bartruhari turned his head slightly and allowed his chin to rest on his left shoulder. But quickly his chin switched over to his right when the youthful voice came from that direction: "Women are very much offended if you are not always ready and in the mood to play the romantic lover."

"You were in the queen's bed only when you were not in a mood to go to your harem... In the queen's bed, you were a door mat...funny, fowl-smelling, dormant like an exhausted warrior. Exhausted warriors have no place by the side of woman longing for the war of love," That was the shaky voice.

"The queen gets lost in the endless deserts of insomnia almost every night. Pity her. Your presence made no difference to her. Blessed is the man who quenches her thirst. Adore him." That was the youthful voice.

Bartruhari was startled by the appearance of a young man at his left who exactly resembled himself. It took no time for him to realise that he had been confronted with himself.

"Tired, my lady?" The stableman's voice distracted Bartruhari and brought him to the world of reality.

The queen, her eyes still closed, cooed: "I felt a warm joy permeate my entire body. It never before happened in my life. You have awakened the woman in me. I can't understand why I have not met you before."

She kissed the stableman with gratitude. She caressed his arm, kissing the nook between the elbows, the shoulders. "The beauty of your arm is exactly like that of your body. If

I didn't know your body, I would want it, just from seeing the shape of your arm." She fondly looked at his arm as if everything she had experienced were but ordeals and this the shelter, the place of happiness.

King Bartruhari envied the man who had charmed his queen. He saw both of them drying their bodies with each other's clothes.

"Moon baths do not make people sweat. Yet these two are profusely sweating. That is the sign of good love making." Bartruhari heard the shaky voice once again.

"If you ever want to be with a man who will readily make love to you, come to me. My service to you, my mare, will be kept as a secret…a secret that will become ashes with me," the stableman said.

The queen, who had experienced the avalanches of the body's tremors, hugged the stableman tight and planted on him kisses wherever her lips could reach. Finally, she arched her body and reached for the thing that penetrated the deepest of her body and planted a long and hearty kiss.

"Think of the night the queen has done that to you, you master of men, women and children. To extract such an act from a woman, all that you need is passion and patience. But you have never found these in your place, be it the palace or the harem," said the shaky voice.

Bartruhari could see the life size image so far standing behind his shrunk inner self walk into him. He then turned to his right. The life size image of the youthful Bartruhari smiled indulgently and before he walked into him said: "Women are what they are. You have to believe them. They are chaste to their chosen man. They can't help being faithful to themselves…to their feelings."

King Bartruhari's mind began to wander between two worlds: one—the world of his queen's feelings; two—the world of internal truth.

His mind began to oscillate like a pendulum, gathering momentum at each swing…faster…faster…and faster.

And as if the pendulum stopped all of a sudden, his mind began to be at peace with himself. Perhaps Truth, the funniest joke in the world, dawned upon him.

He turned back and found no life size image of himself standing anywhere near.

"Truth should be silent," King Bartruhari said to himself, and began walking back to the palace. It was not mad rush, but unperturbed calmness brought him wisdom.

Fathered by pain and mothered by love, wisdom taught him the art of seeing all others' faults and feeling his own.

Bartruhari turned wise in time. By dawn, he donned a saffron robe. In the place of his crown, there was a saffron headgear. His body has disowned all pieces of silver and gold that were hanging on to him till yester-night.

He had no sword or sabre for a sannyasi needs neither of them.

Bartruhari began to trot out of the palace.

"Who is it in the palace at this hour?" The voice was quite familiar to Bartruhari.

He stopped and turned back. The queen's sari was soiled and turds of pressed horse shit showed up here and there. She stank of stable.

The queen smiled and said: "I know…I know this will happen one day. I never knew this would happen so soon."

Bartruhari spoke no word. He maintained a yogic silence.

"I am happy," the queen said and continued, "I am happy that I am instrumental in making an emperor a sannyasi."

"It's not you," retorted Bartruhari. "The credit goes to the stableman."

The queen stared at him full and round. She turned to walk back to her empty bed.

"Wait a minute," Bartruhari said. "When do you intend to make the stableman another sannyasi?"

□

The Wart

Noah stood before a life-size mirror and began shaving himself. It was a sort of ritual he religiously performed everyday before he jumped into a nearby river for a bath. Shaving and bathing were preparations for prayer. And prayer was a starter to go ahead with his daily chores.

A black wart that stood between his left cheek and chin had a lonely grey hair crowning it. In fact, the wart was a real hurdle for the razor to move smoothly and so Noah took extra care when shaving that particular spot for fear of wounding it. He was aware that a bleeding wart would give birth to any number of warts.

A wart symbolises evil. No man born of woman is free from evil. Born with him, it grows with him and dies with him. Only its percentage varies from one man to another. What an ugly thing this wart is on a clean-shaven face! Noah philosophised as he carefully passed the sharp edge of the razor against the wart.

Having shaved himself, Noah turned his face to its left and then to its right and looked keenly into the mirror. Perfect…A clean-shaven face is mark of an immaculate heart. Oh, but for the wart! Every wart is like the tip of an iceberg. Maybe the roots are deep.

Why did this wretched wart of all spots in my body choose my face to show up? Noah thought aloud as he wiped clean his face with a wet towel. He then spread it open and scrutinised it. Tiny particles of grey hair showed themselves up on his brown-coloured towel.

Not a single black particle! God, it speaks of my age. I am like a withering tree soon to become dead wood, only to be burnt and then forgotten. Noah spoke to his image in the mirror. The very thought of dying brought tears to his aged eyes. With the wet towel, he wiped his eyes before the tears could roll down his cheeks.

You are deathless. Good men don't die. Noah heard someone say so. He turned back to see who the speaker was. There was none. The voice continued: They live in others' hearts forever. And you are a good man.

Noah became curious about the invisible speaker. Wanting to know if it was his own image that spoke to him, he looked into the mirror. His image too was equally curious. On further scrutiny, he found a globule of fire inside the mirror that began to expand itself. He once again turned back to know if there was any such fire at his back. He saw no such thing there but the fire in the mirror began to develop into a huge ball of fire.

Panic-stricken Noah knelt down before the mirror. The voice of fire continued: All that is born is to die. And all that is dead is to be burnt and forgotten. Yet some mortals achieve immortality when they prove to be righteous, blameless, and walk with me. This is why I have chosen you.

Chosen me, my God! I can't believe my ears, my God! What good I have done to deserve your blessings, my God? But tell me God, why I am cursed with this black wart for everyone to see?

Be happy and content that it is not there in between your thighs. The voice said and after a pause continued: This is why I consider you good for you have faithfully obeyed my tenth commandment while the rest of men and women neglect this last of my commandments. Mad mongrels…go crazy over flesh. I identify men and women with their warts. It does not look ugly on you as you think it to be. Instead it enhances your charm. Remember a wart is nothing but hard skin meant for easy identification. My angel studied you for years when I assigned him the work of finding out the right sort of man I wanted for my purpose. And when his choice fell on you, he said, a wise man named Noah is that sort of man you are looking for. He added that he could be identified with a black wart on the left side of his face.

Noah expressed dissatisfaction with the God's reply. Convinced that Noah was obsessed with the wart, the God said: I could have given a lot of flesh to hang around your neck; I could have a hillock of flesh on your stomach; I could have given you a big boil on your head to resemble a rhino; I could have given you a lump of flesh on your legs to look like an elephant's.

Before the God could construct another sentence, Noah brought his hands together and crossed his fingers in prayer and said: You are scaring the shit out of me, O God! I do not have any constipation problem, even though you make me put on a constipated look. Let the wart remain as long as it wants to. If it likes my face and wants to grow bigger, let it. I will never again rake up all that muck about this wart.

The wickedness of man is great; his very imagination continually evil. It grieves me to my heart that I have made man on earth. The God's voice was sorrow-stricken.

Too late a realisation, my God! Had you stopped with Adam and refused to lend your ears to his request, this problem of flesh could not have cropped up. I am not wise enough to advise you. Forgive me my God if I sound impertinent. The earth is corrupt and filled with violence; for all flesh had corrupted their way upon the earth.

That's why I have determined to destroy all flesh, for the earth is filled with violence through them. I will blot out man from the face of the earth, man and beast and creeping things and birds, for I am sorry I made them…But I am happy to find the gem among men and so I command you to listen to me and fulfill my wishes.

I am only a shadow of your shadow; breath of your breath. Your word is law to me and I will obey every syllable of it.

This is all that I wanted to hear. Let me hurry up with my command for I have lot of other things to do in Heaven. You are to make an ark of gopher wood, and cover it with pitch. The ark should be four hundred and fifty feet long, seventy-five feet wide, and forty-five feet high. Let the ark have a roof and set the door of the ark in its side; make it with lower, second and third decks. As soon as your ark is ready, I will send a flood upon the earth and make everything perish. But I will establish my covenant with you, and you shall come into the ark with your wife, sons and daughters-in-law. Do not forget to take with you every sort of food and store it up for you and your family and other living beings.

Noah looked inquisitively at the fire in the mirror.

God continued: "Yes! You shall also take two, male and female, of every living thing into your ark, to keep them alive with you…birds, animals and creeping things."

"By creeping things you mean serpent too?"

"Of course, it goes without saying. After my curse in Garden Eden, no snake walks anymore. It is destined to crawl. So, take a pair of them according to their kinds."

Noah pulled a long face. He retorted, "You have not learnt your lessons, God! Why do you want to save the serpent knowing pretty well that it was in every way responsible for the downfall of man? You know that it is the real trouble-maker? And it is because of that wily creeping thing you have thrown man and woman out of your Eden. It is because of that vicious creature man is earning his bread by the sweat of his brows and poor woman brings forth her children in pain."

"True! But your words are incomplete…Did I not favour you when I cursed woman by saying: 'yet your desire shall be for your husband, and he shall rule over you'?"

Noah thought awhile and it took little time for him to understand that God was diverting his attention. "God! I am talking about the snake and you are talking about woman."

God was silent for a minute. Noah smiled and said to himself that God too has to think twice before he makes any comment on snake and woman. "God! Command me to take all the women into the ark. I will gladly do for they deserve to be saved. But it is the serpent I hate. It is the creator of all mischief."

"O mischief! How swift you are to enter in the thoughts of desperate men!" God said in a low tone. And then raising his voice a few decibels, he said: "Noah! To mourn a mischief that is past and gone is the next way to draw new mischief on. Do what I say. Do not question my words."

"Question your words? That's beyond my capacity, God! But please reconsider my request. To have even one serpent is trouble enough. But you want a couple of them in the ark. Please imagine my plight."

"No further doubts and no more questions. Act." With those words the fire in the mirror vanished as quickly as it had appeared.

Noah did all that God commanded him. But he ignored God's advice about taking the serpent couple into the ark. He scrutinised every nook and cranny of the ark by putting to use his olfactory senses. Only when he was convinced that there was no sign of any serpent there, he shut the door of the ark.

There began a heavy downpour of rain. It continued for forty days and forty nights. The waters increased and bore up the ark. Mountains got drowned in the floods. All flesh died. Only Noah and those with him in the ark were left on Planet Earth. God appeared in Noah's dream and said: "Be fruitful." He did not forget to make his appearance in the dream of Noah's daughters-in-law to say "Be fruitful and multiply." Perhaps he said the same to the other animals, birds and creeping things.

On the appointed day he sent one couple after another out of the ark. All animals, birds and creeping things got the blessings from the blessed man and moved out into the world. Noah carefully watched the couples pass by. He ascertained that there was no serpent couple. Joyfully he told his wife, "Now is the time for us to leave the ark. Tell this to our boys and girls. Let them get ready to go out into the world."

Noah's joy knew no bounds when he stood before the life size mirror which he had carefully nailed to a plank inside the ark. He giggled before his own image for he had not shaved himself for nine months. His flowing grey beard and drooping moustaches showed him in a different light. Razor in hand he asked himself: "To shave or not to shave; to keep the ugly wart in hiding behind a bushy growth of hair or to expose it for everyone to see its ugliness after a clean shave; to trim his upper and lower lips or to leave them as such…"

At a time when Noah was seriously thinking of his thick growth of hair, he heard a hiss somewhere nearby. He stood stunned as his razor dropped down to the floor of the ark. Another hiss that followed put him back to his self. He was sure that it was the hiss of a serpent. "My God! How did it manage to get inside the ark when I took all measures to prevent its entry? Is evil so powerful that nothing good on earth can ever destroy it? Evil unchecked is bound to grow. And evil tolerated poisons the whole system…"

Noah searched for a sturdy stick and found one. "I will not allow evil to go out into this new world. Let it die a timely death in the ark itself." Noah waited for another hiss. He sharpened his ears. There came another hiss. He was taken aback for the hiss came from inside the mirror. He moved closer to the mirror. He saw the most venomous serpent king cobra – standing on the tip of its tail and its hood raised and in the same spot where stood the globe of fire months ago.

Noah looked daggers at the serpent. The serpent too reciprocated his anger with a cruel blood-curdling hiss. He tried to wrench his gaze away from the appalling sight.

"What is evil?...Whatever springs from weakness." The words came from behind his back. Swiftly he turned his head back. He found his wife standing there. Noah was flabbergasted. He threw his head back to look for her image in the mirror. He saw only the serpent. Faster he turned his head to see the real serpent. He saw only his wife.

"He who always seeks evil in others finds it." The words of the old woman sent her husband's head reeling.

□

Compassion

How that little creature found its way into the bucket, half-filled with water continued to be a mystery to me. Perhaps it was thirsty and in trying to lick the droplets of water sleeping on the edge of the bucket, the mouse slipped and fell into it. Or was it fate that drew it to the container? I have no answer. Who can ever understand the vagaries of fate?

An hour or so ago, the mouse had the entire world to roam about and feel at home. But now, its world was narrowed down to a bucket, and its freedom curtailed.

It was not yet dawn when I awoke to some scraping sound. With the heaviness of sleep still in my eyes, I cocked up my sharp ears. My detective mind sent signals to every nook and cranny of the entire room and soon found out that the sound came from somewhere nearby. I sharpened my left ear, and pulled the torch light from under my pillow, all in utter silence.

When I ascertained myself that the noise came from just under my bed, I flashed the torch and found the trouble-maker.

It was a mouse trying to eat away a leg of my cot.

The scraping sound came to a sudden halt. The mouse, as if hypnotised by the light, stood blinking with its little red eyes and its wee whiskers glistening.

For a moment, I too felt that I was hypnotised by that inert little creature. And when I came back to myself, the mouse was gone.

A mouse in my house! A creature to be dreaded. One is worth a battalion and I couldn't imagine the fate that awaited my books assiduously collected over the years and stored for my use and for my interested friends as well.

Years ago, a mouse couple had been welcome guests in my study. I didn't bother them since they didn't in any way trouble me. They developed their family in geometric proportions. My wife grumbled when she swept clean the turds off my study, twitching and fending off her nose at the waste those little animals had deposited.

I was no stranger to squeaks and so my wife's grumble passed for yet another squeak. To see my wife slap her forehead as a mark of helplessness was a common sight in those days.

I had no mind to drive away the mice family. What right have I to deny them of their right to stay anywhere in the world!

"All of us, including the family of mice, are only sojourners on this earth," I said philosophically, and saw my wife pull a long face and disappear into the kitchen.

My intimate friends and close colleagues, mostly book lovers, cherished my friendship – for I lent them even the rarest of books without any grudge, on condition that they returned them in time and intact.

Books are after all meant to be read. And by lending books, I do their authors a great service…more number of people read them. I want everyone to follow my principle for I am also an author.

Coming back to the mice family …Oh! I have learnt to live with them in my study, regardless of the noise they made now and then, and the nuisance they created here and there.

But when they wanted to have a taste of my books, I decided to do away with them.

Many a time I have seen my mice hopping over the edges of my books that stood vertically on the shelves. I have seen a trio stretching conveniently and sleeping on the ***Encyclopedia of Dreams***, kept horizontally on the reference shelf. On another occasion, I saw a couple quarreling over Heaven-knows-what on my ***Legal Encyclopaedia***.

No doubt, I delighted my eyes on their life drama. And one day I thanked them profusely when three of my poems, all inspired by them, appeared in an American journal and made me richer by a few dollars.

One Sunday morning, I incurred the wrath of my wife. Now and again I did one thing or another to infuriate her, for she looked more beautiful than ever in that mood. But on that day, it was not me who angered her but my mice.

"You can't have both…your books and your mice… choose between the two," shouted my wife fuming.

I pretended to blink though in my heart of hearts, I was pleased to see her howl like that.

"What is that owlish look for?" She yelled. "Be an owl and eat away all your mice, before they eat away your books."

Startled, I inquired into the matter.

"Hm…The unwanted has happened. Why don't you walk into your study and find for yourself?" she said, arching her eyebrows.

I scurried into my study and there I had the shock of my life.

Shreds of paper collected from underneath the bookshelves kept staring at me.

I bent down to have a closer look at the pile. Then picking up a shred, I looked inquisitively at it.

The colour of the paper and the tiny letters printed on it looked quite familiar. "From what book is that?" I asked myself, and sat on my haunches.

I tried to read the half-eaten words found in the shred but couldn't make any head or tail of it.

I picked up another shred, slightly bigger than the rest in the pile. Luckily two short lines were intact.

The first line read: "What are you reading, my lord?" And the second read: "Words, words, words."

I jumped in joy and cried, "Oh! It's Polonius and Hamlet speaking."

The next minute my joy disappeared and gave rise to sorrow. "Huh! My ***Complete Works of Shakespeare*** edited by Peter Alexander is gone," I screamed.

"Now stop screaming awhile and look at those books I have piled up there, near your writing desk," said my wife over my shoulder, her hand pointing at the direction.

One quick jump. And the pile was at hand. I flipped open a few of them one after the other and found to my dismay that most of the pages in every one of them were gone and the pages that remained were widowed by their 'better-half'.

I turned pale. "Look at what these nasty mice have done to my twenty-volume edition of ***The Arabian Nights***. These books are rare, you know. They are in Sir Richard Burton's translation." I cried.

"Now decide," said my wife authoritatively, "Your books or your mice."

"Definitely my books," I roared. "I'll buy a mousetrap today and see that they are all gone."

"Do not bother. Leave that to me," said my wife, carrying the dustbin away.

The next morning, I entered my study to write an elegy on the untimely death of my Shakespeare and Burton. But...but...

"Hei! What are these black and fluffy little things lying on thc floor?" I yelled calling the attention of my wife busy with the washing machine.

At first I mistook them for lush cobwebs fallen from the loft. But at close quarters, I found that they were all lifeless bodies of the mice, my one-time study mates but now my arch-enemies.

"Oh, my god! It looks like a battlefield. All the villains of my study lie vanquished here. Who has performed this miracle?" I asked.

"Raticide" said my wife entering my study with a long-handled broom in one hand and a plastic bin in the other. For a moment, she looked like a cold-blooded warrior.

"Don't ever think of having mice as your pets again," she said taking a carcass by its tail and throwing it into the bin that began to gulp down the dead mice.

"Twenty-three," said my wife.

"So many! So many in my little study!" I said opening my eyes widely.

"Wait for the grand total...I do not know how many more are lying dead on the loft. There may be some beneath the bookcases and one or two behind them. I'll have to sweep clean your entire study before I give you the exact figure of the dead."

I stood appreciating my duty-conscious wife.

"If you happen to see a live mouse again, don't fail to tell me. I know how much of your money and energy you have spent in making your study what it is today. Don't ever again lose your books to the rats," she warned.

I nodded my head in approval, patting on her shoulder affectionately.

It took several years for me after that crusade on rats to see a mouse again – the mouse that disturbed my sleep but managed its escape.

I remembered my wife's warning and attempted to tell her of the new invader. But my words got strangled in my throat for my wife was not there to hear my complaint.

Jammed between board and glass, she lives in the garlanded photograph on the wall, just above the entrance of my study.

That was why I dreaded the mouse. The creature had set me into thinking all the time about it. "How am I going to dispose it off?" I asked myself repeatedly, still stretched on my lonely bed.

It was only when my mind was struggling to find an answer I saw the mouse in the bucket.

Who did the thinking for me, I do not know.

I sat on my haunches and looked into the bucket.

The mouse was still struggling for its release and I was sure that it could not escape, unless a saviour came to its timely rescue.

Keeping its snout a little above the surface of water, it floated vertically all the time kicking its legs against the water and producing a gleaming circle of ripples. I saw it going down when it became tired and remained motionless. And when water entered its nostrils, it struggled for breath and started kicking once again to reach the surface for a whiff of air.

As I mercilessly watched the mouse struggle with death, the creature looked at me direct into my eyes. It brought its forelegs together now and again. It looked as if it were praying for my mercy. Its eyes seemed to tell me that it had already suffered enough for entering my house and that capital punishment was too much for its intrusion.

As I had not yet lost all compassion for the mouse clan, I rushed into the kitchen and searched for the tongs, with the help of which I could catch the mouse by its neck and carry it to the street and there let it go free…after a strict warning, of course.

But the tongs were playing 'hide and seek' with me and I had to think of another way.

Finding no other alternative, I decided to carry the bucket to the street and splash the water and along with that the mouse on the road.

"Well! Lifc is short for all creatures on earth. Why should I shorten it further for the mouse in the bucket?" so saying I rushed back to the yard.

I was late…perhaps too late.

□

Suicide

Dr. A. Surya Sundari, M.B.B.S., M.S., F.R.C.S. decided to hang herself.

A much-sought-after surgeon both by ailing patients and by doubt-nurturing colleagues, she was a big name in the medical circle. Her younger colleagues always appreciated her and the elder ones patted her on her back for making quick and favourable decisions. And once the decision was made, she never went back on it. In spite of her popularity and affluence, she got ready to move away from this world and she herself was not sure why she took such a decision at that odd hour, and that too all of a sudden.

The preliminaries over, Dr. Surya held the noose in both her hands to widen it so as to push her head into it before she could tighten the noose and kick the stool away.

"So you think your time is over!"

She heard someone say so. Shocked, she let the noose go. She looked around, sideways, up and down to confirm if she was the only one in her bedroom. Ascertaining that she was alone and wondering whose voice it could be, she held the noose again.

"So you think your time is over?"

This time she did not let the noose go off her hands. "Who is that?" She asked in a curt tone.

"Life," came the reply. The word 'life' began to reverberate throughout the room and made her turn her head quickly in different directions.

"Life?" She asked as if she had never heard of that word before.

"Yes… I am Life."

"But where are you?"

"Me? In your hands."

She blinked. She only felt that someone from somewhere was trying to tease her a bit. She looked around again.

"Ha…ha…ha…. You are like any other woman looking everywhere to find me out when I am in your hands."

She thought awhile and then looked at the noose she was holding in her hand.

"Ha! Ha! You are quick-witted. Yes! Life is in your hands."

"What? Is it the noose that is speaking to me?" she asked looking askance at it.

"Why 'Noose'? Call me Life. Don't I make a full circle, and a completed cycle of life?"

Dr. Surya had the shock of her life. She had never before come across a rope or a noose speak to human beings in any of the medical texts she had deeply studied in all these years. She was not sure of any such scene created by writers capable of making anything speak to anyone. Panicky physician pushed the noose away from her with a jerk. It began to swing before her.

"Hold me tight. Don't let Life go off you," said the dangling noose that looked beautiful, integrating and crowning.

She was in a fix. Thoroughly confused, she scratched her head.

"What is there to get confused? Hold me tight. You will learn from me what your parents and teachers, friends and relatives, colleagues and patients have failed. Is not Life, experience incarnate? Hold me tight, tighter than before and do not be afraid of me."

"Pssst…Had I been afraid of you, I would not have touched you with my hands at all?" said Dr.Surya.

"Good! This is what I expected you to say. That is the spirit. An undaunted woman like you should not resort to any base act. I do not know what is going on in your mind but I am sure you are confused if not perturbed."

She realised that Life spoke sense. "Thoroughly confused…yes! I am thoroughly confused," she said as she held the dangling noose in her hand.

"All confusions arise only to be got cleared. Every question has an answer. Every problem is bound to have a solution. If a problem fails to find a solution, then it can't be a problem at all. I would say that you have only failed to find out the solution to your problem. Well, well! I think, I spoke too much. Give me just one reason for taking this stupid decision."

"Reason? You want reason in this unreasonable world?" commented Dr. Surya.

"You are a responsible citizen and you speak in an irresponsible way. We are the creators of our own world and together form one world. Your world may be different from the writer who is telling this story to the world. His would be different from his wife's. Hers would be different from their children's. Yet they make a family. Several families make a nation and several nations make the world. Henceforth, don't blame the world. Blame yourself."

"Blame myself! Why should I blame myself when the world is responsible for driving me to this extreme?" howled Dr. Surya.

"Going to extremes is easy, for people like you suppose that the extreme is the end all of things. But what you call end is no end at all but a new beginning. I wonder why highly educated people like you fail to understand this, when the unlettered easily understand this to the core. Gathering too much of knowledge too is in a way responsible for driving people to extremes," said Life.

"Maybe I had the best in my life right from babyhood to this day. Yet I am confused. Perhaps, I need a new beginning," said Dr. Surya holding the noose in one hand and rubbing her forehead with the other.

"Then begin it. What stops you from starting one anew? From green to greener pastures is the way of life. You are not married all these years. Get married to a man of your choice and spend the rest of your days happily. All human beings need change. In fact, a changeless life is a useless life." Life sermonised.

"Ha…ha…ha…" Dr. Surya laughed like a machine gun at work. "Marriage! Choice! Happiness! All balderdash. Not one goes hand in hand with the other. Not that I had not thought about them when I was quite young. I have seen the way of the world and there can be no harmony between man and woman, especially with the highly educated ones. My parents too were physicians and they loved only each other's money. Not a day passed without a quarrel and that may be the reason for my being their only child. I don't want to be harassed by a stranger. I have seen enough in my lifetime. No man loves his spouse with all his heart. Neither does the woman. Marriage is a failure in many western countries. That is why divorcing one's spouse is quite easy. But here in our country it is the most difficult of all. How long can one tolerate the other? What can be more boring than marital ties?"

"Well then! How about an affair with a man of your choice?" asked Life without a moment's hesitation and suggested, "There is nothing wrong in it. In a way it is better than marriage. And responsibility too is nil."

"Hm… You seem to have read my mind," said Dr. Surya. "Once I thought of that too. And that was years ago when I met my match. He was a professor and writer. When I met him, I was as old as his eldest sister. Unfortunately, he was married and was living with a lovely wife and two cute little kids. That was the time when I thought of an affair with him. No man but an impotent says no to any woman when it comes to joys of the flesh. But I soon realised that I can't play second fiddle to anyone. An affair is fatal relationship. I can't afford to risk my precious life for the sake of seven minutes of pleasure."

"You speak as though they are seven deadly sins. If you are not interested in a man for any sort of relationship, then you could have very well adopted a child from an orphanage...say, a girl child," said Life and, without waiting for her answer, continued, "It is your loneliness that drove you to hug death. I hope you agree with me."

Dr. Surya was silent awhile and then said, "Thank you very much for your concern. I do not agree with you. Nor do I disagree with you. Your question is quite blunt. The idea of adopting a child flashed across my mind once. But somehow the idea continued to remain without any action, for, on second thoughts, I found that I would not be a good mother to the child. I learnt these lessons from my dead mother. The wounds that my parents left in me are beyond healing. They are perennial blisters and I don't want to be responsible in any way for leaving even the slightest scar in anyone's heart."

Life laughed to its heart's content. Dr. Surya looked at the noose with probing eyes.

"You have left very many scars on your patients!" mocked Life.

"Of course, I did. My profession demanded it. I couldn't help it. Scar is history. Blister is news." She giggled before she added, "A touch of women's rights here."

"But no law will ever give you the right to take away your life," said Life in all humility.

"Ha...ha...Haven't you heard of mercy killing? Nobody can stop me when I decide to practise it on myself." She laughed with a flash of delight, as if an unexpected boon had fallen into her lap.

"Stooping to the mercy of a killer when Life has endowed you with the knowledge to save lives is something unpardonable. Think it over and find out what is responsible for your malaise," advised Life.

"I told you I don't know what it is that drives me to this end. I only know that I am not what I am. Leave me to myself. Let me die," said she in a fit of fury.

"That's what I want you to do. Die to be born anew. Only you can kill that malaise in you. Shed it like a snake that sloughs off its skin. And that is why I have given you so many suggestions," said Life patiently.

"But you are too boring. I think I have lived enough here..."

Before Dr. Surya could complete her sentence, Life interrupted her and said, "Then take a trip abroad for a change. That is also a best way of relaxation. You have worked too much. It is monotony of work that is killing you. Go to some country you have so far not visited. In spite of your wide travels, I am sure there must be some country in the world that your feet have not graced."

"Only the moon," she said with her head held high. "I have no intention of going there for I know what is there. But as you say, I will visit the country of my choice...the undiscovered country. So, leave me alone, please."

"Look! You are only holding me. I leave you to your fate. I took all possible efforts to dissuade you from committing this sin. You do not heed my words. It is useless to talk to the educated mankind. I feel sorry for having wasted my time on you. I have a hundred and one things to do and yet I rushed to counsel you. Fiasco...utter fiasco. If a woman takes a decision, nothing on earth can stop her from doing it. So, feel free. I will not be there to stop you. Go to that undiscovered country you want to visit but rest assured that no traveller to that country ever returned," said Life.

"Ha." Dr. Surya let out a short cough. "You don't have to teach me all that. Now go and mind your business," she said bluntly.

Life felt defeated, humiliated in front of his exciting adult friend whose life he wanted to extend. He left the noose and turned round at the door with a scowl. Before he disappeared from the scene, he said, "How do you know that worse things are not waiting for you there?"

Life's last words kept reverberating in Dr. Surya's ears for hours together till her stomach growled and whined with hunger. Its unending protest made her embarrassed to stand before the noose.

□

The Sinner

Reverend Father Antonisamy paused, wiping the sweat from his face with his hanky. He adjusted his cassock as his entire body was swathed in sweat. It was the hottest summer evening and there was an unexpected power failure. The heat was nearly unbearable, but the sweating mass in the St. Francis of Assisi Church at Kurusukuppam eagerly awaited his sermon to continue. He caved in his lower lip and covering it with his upper one, blew out air and redirected it inside his cassock.

"Let me proceed," he said, "Now that I have come to the end of the sermon, there is no need to stop at this juncture... And so Jesus is a symbol...a symbol of peace and love. He is the image of the invisible God, the first born of all creation; for in him all things were created...all things were created through him and for him. He is before all things, and in him all things hold together. Let the word of Christ dwell in you richly, teach and admonish one another in all wisdom, and sing songs and hymns with thankfulness in your hearts to God. And whatever you do, in word or deed, do everything in the name of the Lord Jesus, giving thanks to God the Father through him...Amen."

"Amen," chorused the gathering inside the church and knelt down to pray. Father Antonisamy raised both his hands towards heaven and recited a prayer. As he sang a line from the Lord's prayer and paused, the gathering chorused by repeating that line. It went on like this, line after line, and finally came to a halt with the all-powerful word 'Amen'.

The nearby sea, as if desirous of answering their prayer, blew a chill cool wind inside the church and it was a real relief to every one of them. "That's the result of mass prayer," said Father Antonisamy.

The congregation moved towards Father Antonisamy to receive his blessings. As one after the other genuflected before him, he too blessed them by drawing a cross on their forehead with his right thumb. There was no visible queue but every one of them waited for their turn.

A young man dressed differently from the rest of the Kurusukuppam villagers, who mostly depended on the sea for a living, gave way to the rest as if he wanted to meet the priest at the end of the blessing session.

Dressed in half white full-sleeved shirt tucked in khaki-coloured trousers, the young man looked trim like a military official. His dark hair, cut close to his skull only added to it. When he found no one around, he genuflected before the priest and closed his eyes.

Father Antonisamy smiled and his eyes twinkled. His immaculate white cassock sat glued to his profusely sweating body. He crossed the forehead of the young man and hurried out of the church for a whiff of fresh air. The youngman followed him.

The priest stood in the shade of a huge neem tree. He pulled out his hanky from the side pocket of his cassock and wiped his face hard. His clean-shaven face glowed. He saw the young man walk towards him. As the latter brought both his hands together and saluted the former in the traditional way, the priest nodded his head acknowledging the respect shown to him.

"Do you remember me, Father?" the young man asked.

Father Antonisamy observed him at close quarters and said, "You are the last in the list of those who received my blessings for the day."

"That's right, father! But apart from that…Can you recognise me?" The young man grinned and looked around him anxiously.

The priest concentrated on the facial features of the young man. He then said softly, "Why do you want to play 'hide and seek' with me? Why don't you come out?"

"Six years ago, you got me a seat in St. Joseph's College to study Physics. I am now a postgraduate and I have a job in Delhi," said the young man.

"Oh, I see!" said the priest and smiled. "And what are you in Delhi?"

"I am a scientist, Father," he answered and beamed a smile.

"A scientist! Good…That's good. This is something I can feel proud of…I am really proud of you, my son," said Father Antonisamy, before he asked, "What is the nature of your job?"

The youngman looked around him anxiously. "Are we alone, Father?"

Father Antonisamy looked at him silently for one full minute and then said, "I think so."

"Fine. That's the first rule. You hear from me and then you forget all that I say. When I finish telling you, I cease to exist for you. I think I have made myself clear to you."

"I understand."

"Our key word is: Secrecy." He took a couple of forward steps and positioned himself in such a manner that his lips could easily touch the priest's right ear. He then whispered, "Father! By the grace of Jesus, our Lord, I hold an enviable position in the Defence Force."

"Excellent…excellent…I am really proud of you," said the priest. He then added, "Certainly it is by the grace of Jesus, our turning point in life."

"Yes, Father! I work as a designer."

"Designer! What do you design?"

"I design weapons, Father. I heard my superiors say that I am very good at it. By the grace of Jesus, I design two to three weapons a year."

"Weapons! You mean killer machines?" queried the priest.

"Yes, Father! We redesign so that the old ones will go out of use. By the grace of our Lord, our new machines work faster than their seniors."

Father Antonisamy could almost see the image of the young man beginning to crumble.

"By the grace of our Lord Jesus, I make a lot of…"

"Stop it," the priest said brusquely. "It is hardly worth mentioning." He then raised both his hands towards heaven and his lips mumbled: "By the grace of our Lord, let peace prevail on this earth and let the lamb and the lion eat together."

Father Antonisamy's arms dropped and he edged his way to the door of the church again and plodded his way to the cross, and knelt down. He joined both his hands in prayer. His head bent down, he prayed as if he were making a confession before a parish priest for the sin he had committed six years ago.

Tears threatened to trickle out of his eyes.

□

Best for the Occasion

Little Auro giggled. He tried to suppress the giggle but burst into laughter and thereby attracted the attention of his mother.

Auro's mother, enamoured of a painting in the art gallery, was about to take off on the viewless wings of poesy, when her son's rocking laughter pulled her back. She looked at her ten-year-old bony boy. She has not seen him laugh like that for a very long time. At first, she ran her eyes around to locate the target of the boy's laughter. She failed. Smiling she asked, "What is it, Auro?"

Her delicate voice perhaps got drowned in the noise of the boy's laughter. He didn't seem to take note of his mother's anxiety. Her motherly eyes didn't fail to take notice of the change in the boy's face.

Less than three years ago, when she was in Trivandrum to attend a friend's wedding, she snatched a few hours from her tight schedule to go around a zoo to pleasure the child. Holding her hand, Auro moved from cage to cage watching birds and animals that he had seen only in 'Animal Planet' channel of the TV, one among the few channels he was allowed to watch after his school hours. He was able to identify several creatures of God and name them too. Auro's scholarly mother proudly looked at her son at such times and smiled to herself. He was having fun time with almost every inhabitant of the different cages. But his face all of a sudden changed colour when they reached a differently built cage open to the sky. Auro's eyes frantically searched for this cage dweller but couldn't spot out any creature, except a few stray crows pecking at the left-over and cawing to express their satisfaction.

Auro looked inquiringly at his mother who too betrayed ignorance. When they were about to move to the next cage, out emerged an animal from an artificial pool whose water looked as though it were from Aegean Stable. Smooth, shiny and soft was its skin as though neatly shaven by a skilled barber. Not a drop of water managed to find shelter on its huge, unshapely and so ugly body.

It was a hippo. Its funny face attracted the boy and he laughed aloud to his heart's content. Perhaps attracted by the child's innocent laughter, the animal ambled towards him. It then turned sideways and exhibited its shiny body. The child stopped laughing. Curiosity drove him to take closer looks at the animal. The animal began to wag its funnily short tail sideways gathering greater momentum that made every onlooker imagine that it was going to fritter and break. Then all of a sudden, the tip of the tail looked up at the sky and became motionless. The animal's huge belly caved in for a second or two, and then it let out a long fart.

Several people guffawed. A few held their nose tight with a couple of their fingers and moved away in disgust. Auro's mother too smiled while the boy began to laugh continuously till his face changed colour and he started coughing incessantly before he swooned.

She didn't want that to recur for she couldn't afford to undergo that trauma all over again. And so inside the art gallery, she shook Auro by his shoulder. "Stop it, Auro! What is it this time?" she asked in a stern voice.

Auro's laughter began to wane and finally he showed the artist standing in one corner of the gallery and briefing an inquisitive listener about his recent painting he had displayed for sale there.

She looked at the artist. His shirt was sleeveless and looked as though the sleeves were forcibly torn from its main body. His branded shorts had a couple of holes big enough for any grown-up mouse to enter through one and come out of the other. His shirt barely reached his hip and looked as though he were wearing his little brother's.

"Does he tickle you to laughter?" she asked. A smile flitted across her face.

Auro nodded his head. He was sure that his mom didn't like the way he laughed. "He would easily pass for a beggar to others. But to me he is a comic figure," he said.

She stared Auro's eyes down. "Look Auro! He is a famous painter and..."

"So what?" Auro interrupted her and said, "I have seen short films on artists and painters on History and Discovery Channels. Every great Italian painter, like his counterpart in the other parts of the globe, is well dressed. But is this man so poor that he can dress only shabbily?"

"Listen Auro! Painters and artists rarely care for their external appearance," she said curtly and before she could continue to speak in favour of them, Auro's attention got diverted. Her eyes meandered towards the direction that attracted her son's attention.

There entered a middle-aged woman sparsely dressed. She was exhibiting her gifts from god in all possible places of her anatomy. As she sailed across the hall, she cooed: "Hi, everybody! I am Udhpa Dupha, the famous painter from Sri Lanka. Twenty-five of the sixty paintings displayed in this art gallery are mine. I hope you like them. Please do not forget to register your comments in the notebook at the counter." As she jogged her way along, the hearts of youngsters gathered there bobbed up and down to the tune of her dancing breasts.

Auro pouted out his lower lip and displayed his contempt for her. "Don't you feel like laughing at her dress, mom?"

"Listen Auro! Haven't you seen the picture of Einstein, the great scientist? He never had his shaggy hair combed. Haven't you seen photographs of Mahatma Gandhi? Is he dressed from head to toe? I told you half-a-dozen times that great men and women rarely care for their physical appearance. They have a special kind of impressiveness, resulting from the combination of great intellect with child-like simplicity. So, stop laughing at them and try to appreciate their hard labour that have gone into the making of these beautiful, lovely and charismatic paintings. Learn to appreciate others. You too have bagged prizes in the painting competitions. If you develop that art, you will one day be a good painter like these who joined hands to exhibit their talents here."

Auro turned his head away from his mother and mumbled: "Aren't you a writer?"

"Yes! Of course, I am!" she replied in pride and looked inquisitively at her son. She was not sure of the next question her intelligent son was about to shoot at her.

"But, mom!" continued Auro, "I have never seen you dress in the way they do."

His words silenced her for a minute. Yet she has to wriggle out of the situation. "But I am a professor too! You know, Auro, I have to face several students in classrooms everyday. And they are mostly boys."

"So what?" Auro sounded arrogant.

"What do you mean 'so what'?" She was equally arrogant.

"Mom! You only told me that painters and artists do not care for external appearance." Auro sounded polite.

"Yes! I did." She was equally polite.

Finding that his mother has cooled down, Auro shot his next question. "Writers like you belong to that category or not? Don't say 'no' mom! If painters use brush, you writers use pen to paint pictures in words."

She thought for a moment for she couldn't guess what her son was up to. She began to use words cautiously. "Yes! They do, provided they are full-time writers; provided they are not teachers in a school or college."

"What goes wrong if they are one, mom?"

"Hm…you see, Auro!" She began to fumble for an answer but finally managed with one. She said, "A teacher is looked upon as a model to be followed by the taught. Painters, artists and writers are of a different mould. The more famous they become, the more eccentric they are. Their eccentricity adds charm to their personality. And they do not fear public opinion. This may not hold true for people in the teaching profession. I hope you understand." She moved to a nearby cafeteria with the intention of avoiding his further questions and ordered for chocolate ice-cream to silence the inquisitive boy.

It was past nine when mother and son reached home. On their way back home, they stopped at a Chinese restaurant and had their favourite chicken noodles and fish roe for supper. Auro never knew what hunger was. And his mother never grudged opening her purse for him.

"Change your dress Auro and go to bed," she said, as she opened her wardrobe to pull out a nightie for herself.

As she emerged out of the room, she saw Auro dressed in his best. For a second, she couldn't believe her eyes. He looked as though he were about to move on to a stage to receive an international award.

"You look grand in this, Auro! But why this dress at this hour? You can put it on when you accompany me to the next painting exhibition or book release function.

Auro hee-hawed and then said, "I have the best clothes for such occasions."

"What? You mean you have better clothes than this?" She shot a suspicious glare at him.

"Hm…Definitely the best for such occasions," Auro confirmed and showed the bundle of clothes dumped in one corner of the room. They were yet to be discarded.

They were Auro's old clothes, mostly worn out by years and torn or showing up at the seams. He had outgrown them all.

"I will pass for a famous young painter, mom!" Auro said with a smile. His mother had no way but to grin sheepishly.

□

The Black Bitch

The bitch looked quite different. Different because it didn't bark at me as is expected of its clan before strangers. Neither did it wag its tail. At first, it looked at me as if I were from another world. I was a bit perturbed for I was a stranger to that place. Then it simply ignored me by looking in a different direction.

I couldn't take another forward step for the bitch was close by the gate of my rented house I was yet to occupy. An unexpected transfer brought me to Karaikal and a colleague of mine procured a good-looking house in a decent locality, by name Nehru Nagar. It was quite close to the college in which I joined duty as an English teacher. And so without second thoughts, I took the key from the landlord.

The bitch was a real threat to me. Barking dogs seldom bite, they say. But how about this bitch that is indifferent? Having assisted my grandmother while she treated patients of dog bite with her miraculous herbs, I was sure of what dogs were capable of.

I looked intently at the bitch. It looked neither ferocious nor friendly. It was bluish black in colour and not a single hair on its healthy body sported a different hue. Its ears were very long and its tail curved up to a point in a miniature sickle. "Oh, God! It will be invisible in the dark," I said to myself and decided to carry torchlight whenever I ventured out. Its amber eyes, I was sure, would reflect the light.

As I was involved in the thoughts of befriending the bitch, a milkman pedalled his way through the street pressing the air-horn attached to the handlebar of his bicycle. Pee…po…pee…po…pee…po.

To my great surprise, the bitch imitated the sound of the air-horn as meticulously as a human being would. I couldn't but admire the bitch for its imitative skills.

The sound of the air horn-pulled out many of my neighbours from their respective houses, each one holding a vessel.

I smiled at every one of them and nodded my head in order to introduce myself and get introduced. But that morning hour would not allow any man or woman to be out of their houses. One smiled back, two ran back into their homes without responding and one was all the time looking at the ground.

My immediate neighbour stood for a time, adjusted her sari and then asked me: "Are you my new neighbour?"

I bobbed my head up and down.

"I am told that you are an English professor?" She asked.

"Yes, Madam," I replied with a gleam in my eyes.

"When are you shifting?" she asked.

"I am moving in now, Madam. My luggage will reach me in a day or two," I replied.

"Hm…by luggage you mean your wife and children?" She asked with a smile.

"No, no! By luggage I meant only luggage," I answered smiling back.

"Aren't you married?" She probed further.

"Of course, I am. I have three kids. But in Karaikal, I will have to lead the life of a forced bachelor," I said and added, "I will be with my family on weekends."

"Oh, I see! Are you a vegetarian or non-vegetarian?" she asked me as if she were the landlady and I destined to answer all her questions.

"I am a pure non-vegetarian, Madam," I said with a toothy smile.

"Then this Blackie will be yours forever. She rarely eats the leftovers from our houses. We are all vegetarians as you can notice from our looks," she said.

The cooker from her kitchen whistled. "Oh, I have to rush now. Come home, Professor, when you are free," she sailed back into her house as her words sailed back towards me.

I emboldened myself to take my forward step. The bitch didn't stir. Perhaps it was in a dreamy state thinking of where it could get the next bone.

The milkman went to the dead end of the street and returned, all the time pressing the air-horn.

The bitch that so far maintained a yogic silence began to imitate again: Pee…po…Pee…po…pee…po…

The milkman got down from his vehicle, parked it on its stand, searched for a coconut shell, found one, cleaned it with his hands, blew the dust off it and then poured milk into it to its brim.

The bitch looked at the milkman, but did not wag its tail. It moved aside giving way for me to reach the gate.

"She is special to me, sir! I can't afford to keep a pet at home. She is very mischievous but has never harmed anyone. Can't see such a pious dog anywhere in Karaikal. I love her, sir!" certified the milkman.

I smiled as I unlocked the main gate of the house.

"Shall I supply you milk from tomorrow, sir?" he asked.

I smiled at him and said, "I will let you know."

"Okay, sir," said the milkman, as he jumped on to his bicycle. He then said, " You too will love every action of Blackie, sir. Have a good day."

As I slipped the key into its hole and clicked it open, Blackie was slurping the milk up…. A couple of dogs sauntered past her with their tails tucked between their hind legs. They claimed no share of the milk.

I took an undue interest in the bitch for reasons known only to the celestial beings. Since I cooked my own meals,

I made it a point to feed Blackie twice a day. As I myself skipped breakfast to keep a fast developing tummy under control, I offered her only disappointment in the mornings.

I was in for a big surprise on the first night I brought food out of my house on a leaf plate. The plate was full of gravy-mixed rice with a lot of chicken bones with stray flesh still sticking to them. I placed it carefully under a nearby tree and expected Blackie to wag her tail as a mark of gratitude. But the bitch stood up, stretched herself, yawned and then all of a sudden took to her heels.

"What? You think I am poisoning you, eh?" I asked. But by the time I could finish the sentence, Blackie was out of my sight.

I waited there for a few more minutes. Half-a-dozen dogs that were having a jolly good time in playing and teasing each other, slowed down their steps as they neared my house. One of them, perhaps, attracted by the smell of food waiting to be eaten, strayed away from the pack. But another dog, bigger in size, reprimanded it with a sharp yell. The dog that strayed sharply turned and joined back its friends. And all of them went away without letting out a yell or a bark.

"Strange are the ways of these dogs." It was my loud thinking.

"Hi, Professor! Feeding Blackie?" asked the lady of the next door.

I nodded my head.

"Why don't you open your mouth and speak, Professor?" she said with a giggle.

I was sure that she was desirous of involving me in a conversation. She was only a few yards away. I moved closer to her. What separated us was only the compound wall of her house that reached to our chests.

"Yes, Madam," I said.

"Stop calling me Madam. I am Padmasani. You can call me Padma," she introduced herself.

I giggled.

She looked suspiciously at me.

For fear that she would misread my giggle, I said, "I hope no one calls you by the other half of your name, except perhaps your hubby when angry."

She broke into a peal of laughter, showing all her healthy and well-arranged teeth.

"Hm…you are full of humour," she complimented. "Well! Jokes apart, don't expect Blackie to eat in your presence. She is shy of men," she said with a wink.

"Unbelievable," I said.

"There are so many things that you can never believe about Blackie. She is a legend here. You will get to know more about her as time passes," Padma said. As she continued feeding her grandchild seated on her voluptuous hip from a silver bowl filled with cooked and meshed rice, ghee and dhal, she added: "Please come home for tea tomorrow."

An hour or so later, I went up to the terrace to walk a bit before I flopped into bed to hug sleep. Once on the terrace, I heard the sound of munching and crunching of bones coming up from the street. I leaned over the parapet and saw Blackie feasting on what I left under the tree.

She had almost finished eating when perhaps her doggy sense told her that someone was watching. She looked up at me, running her tongue all over her mouth. She then whined and looked in different directions. Ascertaining that there was no one around, she continued gobbling up.

On the morning of the next day, I carried my garbage can to empty it in the dump, a stone's throw away from my house. Blackie followed me, without a bark or wag of its tail.

No sooner did I near the dump than a dozen or more sleeping dogs stood up startled. Later I understood from sheer observation that five o'clock in the morning was too early for the people of Karaikal to be out of bed. In Pondicherry, one can see women sprinkle water and draw kolams in front of their houses well before daybreak and this they do ceremoniously to give a grand gala welcome to the rising sun. But in Karaikal, these things happen not before seven. Early to bed and late to rise, seems to be part of their credo.

It was no wonder that the dogs saw in me a stranger loitering at that unexpected hour. They began to bark in a chorus and were perhaps preparing to attack me.

Blackie growled.

A sepulchral silence prevailed and all the dogs disappeared without a trace.

While sipping tea with Padma in her house on that evening, I narrated how Blackie played guardian angel to me.

"I told you, you know, Professor! She loves you," Padma said with a stress on the four-letter word with layers and layers of meanings.

I tried to suppress my laughter. Seeing me struggle, Padma broke into a guffaw and I could see her eyes glitter.

"Blackie is very pious, you know," Padma said in an attempt to change the topic.

"What?" I asked because I could not resist the temptation of probing into the matter.

"Yes, Professor. She prays everyday," she said and after a pause added, "It is to be seen to be believed."

"No, Padma! Blackie is of a different mould, different from the rest of the canines I see in Nehru Nagar," I said, expressing gleefully my discovery.

"And Nehru Nagar is infested with street dogs. It is dangerous to go out after dark," Padma added.

"Infested? How many approximately?" I asked as fear began to grip me.

"There are six crosses in Nehru Nagar…not less than a hundred houses in each cross. I am sure that each cross feeds a minimum of twenty-five dogs," Padma gave statistics.

"Why not give a complaint to the municipal authorities? The dog catchers will be here," I suggested.

"Oh no! The dogs are the real policemen of Nehru Nagar. Not a theft was reported here so far," Padma said with a lot of concern for the dogs.

A week or so later, I experienced the truth in what Padma had said.

I was returning home after watching a late night horror movie in Shamina theatre, in the vicinity of Nehru Nagar. The time was an hour or so past midnight and I was on foot.

I crossed the first main road and took the street that connected all the six crosses. When I reached the third cross, a stray dog let out a blood-curdling howl. And God knows where from they came…they came in a battalion and sent a chill down my spine. My body began to shake as the barking pack came galloping towards me.

I was told that the best way to face dogs was with stones. But wisdom told me to remain inert. I was not sure what portion of my dear flesh would be mine after everyone had his or her share of the booty.

Blackie too must have been there for I heard her growl and all the dogs as if obeying the command of a captain traced back their steps leaving me to myself.

I heaved a sigh of relief. From that night onwards, no dog dared bark at me. I felt I was special to them.

Watching Blackie and her day-to-day activities became my pastime. I was surprised at her talent for mimicry. Every time the milkman came to our street, she mimicked the pee…po…pee…po…sound of the air-horn.

No hawker's voice ever posed any problem to Blackie. She was always at the heels of the fisherwoman who carried a basketful of fish on her head and whenever she cried *meenu…meenu…* Blackie reproduced the first syllable of the word and stretch it beyond measure. To see her mouth go in different directions in her attempt to pronounce the syllable is to be seen rather than described.

Blackie's favourite was a greens vendor. He used to come pushing a cart loaded with all sorts of greens and country vegetables. And when he cried *keerai...keerai*, she simply repeated the words, of course, in her doggy accent.

And on one Sunday, when I was at home relaxing in an easy chair spread on the sit-out and reading an excellent book on animals titled ***Wonderful People*** by Dr. Howl L. Barker, the call for prayer from a nearby mosque broke the silence.

Blackie mimicked the voice of the muezzin in the way it was uttered. At first I thought it was a kid trying to imitate the muezzin. I rushed out to admonish the child. To my great surprise, I saw Blackie standing on its hind legs and repeating the voice from the mosque.

"I told you, you know! Blackie is a very pious bitch," said Padma, standing and watching Blackie pray, "Be it the clink clanking of bells from the temple, or the gong from the church or the call for prayer from the mosque Blackie mimics and that is her prayer."

Padma's words made me think highly of Blackie for what bitch knows about religion and think that all religions are one and the same and that there is only one God for the whole universe.

My quota of food for Blackie went up.

I was sure that I had disappointed Blackie for nearly four weeks when I was away in Pondicherry enjoying the holidays after semester exams.

On Fridays before sun down, I used to pack my sling bag and start for the Nehru Nagar bus stop to catch a bus to Pondicherry. On such days, Blackie was unhappy and expressed her disappointment by rolling over on its back on the street like an adamant child and whimpered till I disappeared from her sight.

And on Monday mornings, the moment she sighted me, she expressed her joy by running hither and thither on the street regardless of the careless two-wheelers.

After the vacation, I reached back Nehru Nagar. I found no dog...not a single one.

Where have they all gone?

There was no one in the street to answer my question. And then I too have forgotten all about the dogs.

Three days later, when I was returning from a colleague's house in the sixth cross, I found a bitch lying curled up near the street corner. It was Blackie.

"Hi, Blackie! Nice to see you back," I said and moved towards the bitch. She looked gravely from one side to the other for a moment and then dropping her chin on her paw closed her eyes with a grunt of discontent.

Not willing to leave her at that, I bent down, pawed her head and in a cajoling tone said, "Come on, Blackie! I have food for you…"

Blackie rose to her heels with a start, growled and bared her teeth at me and threatened to tear my flesh.

Nervous, I drew back in fright. Blackie growled again and ran as fast as ever.

Everything remained a mystery to me till Padma came home with sweets and snacks that she had brought from her in-laws in Kerala.

Padma talked at length of how much she missed my company and what urgent call from Kerala made her rush to that place a few days ago.

"Oh God! What a tedious journey! I am dog tired," Padma said amidst a huff and a puff.

I was reminded of the dogs in Nehru Nagar. I asked her what had happened to them.

"Huff…The chairman of Nehru Nagar Landlords' Association complained to the municipal authorities. The dog catchers did their job very well and carried every one of them away," Padma said in a dull voice. She shuddered but looked away.

"But I saw Blackie a few days ago," I said.

Padma was silent for a time. I saw a tear drop or two trickle out of her eyes.

"They came in three vans…these dog catchers," Padma began. "They parked their vehicles in three different corners of Nehru Nagar. And several men, all khaki clad, plunged into action. Throughout the day, Nehru Nagar was reverberating with yelps and whimpers of dogs. I saw our Blackie too inside the van parked in the shade of the tree in front of your house." Padma paused.

"So you bribed the bitch catcher and pulled Blackie out," I interrupted.

"No, Professor, no," she said. "That is the interesting part of the story. Just before sundown, there was a call for prayer from the mosque. Blackie stood on her hind legs, brought her forelegs together and imitated in her doggy accent the voice of the muezzin.

"My God! And then?" I sounded curious.

"And then…the driver of the van admiring at Blackie's piety told one of the catchers to pull her out and release her. The catcher too very much pleased with the doings of the bitch allowed her to live long. And this is how she is here, while all her friends and mates by this time would have reached Heaven," Padma said.

She then continued: "But Blackie is dead wood now. I am told that she refuses to take food…always thinking of her lost companions. She is a different Blackie now."

"She is always different," I said suppressing a tear threatening to spill over.

□

Sorrow of Sanity

Professor Arasu parked his car in front of his house but hesitated to get down. Something in him stopped him from doing so. He was a straightforward man and took little time to take decisions. And once he took his decisions, he never went back on them. Yet on that particular day, he wavered to push open the car door.

The little 'glitsch' sound that came from under the car sent tremours down his spine. He was sure that something alive got crushed under his wheels. The very thought of it made him dizzy and uncomfortable.

To say that Arasu is a pure vegetarian would only amount to exaggeration. In fact, he is a connoisseur of good food and spends a fortune in getting them on his table. He is one among those who believe in the saying: "The sin of killing gets washed down the gullet once the killed is eaten."

Once when he was heading for his house on his motorcycle after visiting a friend in a village, a cock flew from somewhere and got hit by the speeding wheels and became immobile. Professor Arasu had no regrets. He picked up the dead cock and carried it home to make chicken soup.

Arasu was sure that it was not a fowl that got crushed by his car.

During his boyhood days, Arasu's father never said 'no' to him and he got him all that he wanted just for the asking. Wild rabbit, mynah, love birds, white rats were brought home to be Arasu's pets. And along with the pets, Arasu's father brought in skilled carpenters and made beautiful cages to house the pets. He was happy to see his son wallow in joy.

One of his favourite pets, a white rabbit, once fell a prey to a stray dog. The dead rabbit was kept in the same position till Arasu came back home in the evening after school. At the very sight of his dead pet, Arasu screamed, cried and howled, and thereby created such a scene that the entire village gathered in front of his house to console the bereaved boy.

On another occasion, he helplessly watched a cat carry away his pet parrot while the bird screeched for help in human tongue. The pitiable sight of the pet got so deep into his heart that he fell sick and had to be absent from school for days together.

Arasu never loved to have a cat or a dog for his pet. His father had once told him of a French lady by name Madame Monier, who was willing to give away an Alsatian pup in exchange for a male wild rabbit of his. But all that his father got from Arasu was a scream and a howl. And his father had to cut a sorry figure before Madame Monier for not fulfilling her desires.

Arasu's refusal to have a dog or a cat at home as his pet should not be construed that he had no love for them. He never hurled a stone at them. He never poured boiling water on them. That was proof enough to show that he had no hatred for them.

Arasu had gone all the way to Velankanni Church to marry a girl of his mother's choice. And on his way back home in a taxi with his newly wedded wife, the taxi driver mercilessly killed all the stray dogs that crossed his way.

At first Arasu took them for accident. But when the driver did it for the third time, Arasu was a bit shocked. In a perturbed tone, he told the driver: "Your rash driving makes many a dog lose their lives.."

The driver guffawed. "Auspicious days demand sacrifices, sir," he said casually without slowing down his speed.

Arasu lost his temper and gave a bit of his mind to the driver. As a professor, he invariably lectured to his students that castes and religions were all man-made; there can be only one force that can rule the world; and all the stupid beliefs have to be erased from the earth.

Imagine what would happen to such a man if one talks of blood sacrifice. The driver found himself in a quagmire of silence. Broken hearted, he slowed down his speed and could not raise it above 40 km per hour. At the sight of a stray dog at a distance, he had no way but bring down his speed further and helplessly watch cyclists overtaking his taxi.

Such was the love our professor showed to stray animals on the streets. Buses, lorries and other heavy vehicles that mercilessly commit daylight murders and also murders in the dark under the pretext of accidents have given him sleepless nights.

What if it is a cat or a rat? A life is a life. When we can show a lot of sympathy towards a man killed by a speeding vehicle, what deters us from having such a feeling when it comes to stray animals? That was our professor's philosophy and question.

Hence, it was no wonder that the crushing sound he heard from under his car disturbed his heart to its very auricles and ventricles.

But how long can one afford to hide inside a car? Mustering up all his courage, he put his right foot out and bent himself sideways and turned his head as far as he could stretch. He then began his search. He could find nothing. He then bent down even to the verge of breaking his backbone and looked at the two wheels to his right. He found nothing.

He sniffed like a police trained dog to know if that spot smacked of fresh blood. His olfactory senses could not detect anything of that sort.

With stupid confidence, he placed his other foot too out and got out of his car and banged its door shut.

He then took just two steps forward towards the back of his car. His feet got arrested. At least that was what he thought. The sight was quite unbearable. And his face turned pale.

Something was found lying there like a pouch, used by oldies half-a-century ago meant for carrying in it betel leaves, nuts, the round quarter anna with a big hole in it, the square half anna and the curve edged one anna.

Two further steps…he felt as if a little ray of lightning were crossing his body.

Poor thing! It was a dead cat. A very young one at that…may be a month old.

Arasu felt a sharp pain darting deep into his heart; a deep sense of guilt entered him. His mind was so thoroughly confused that he felt as though his heart got pounded in an electrical mixing jar.

Unable to bear the sight of the kitten lying almost folded twice, he walked into his house and fell on the sofa with a thud. The sponge too turned hard like a stone for him. He stretched his legs forward and leaned back and rested his head on the top spine of the seat. As if unable to face the world, he closed his eyes.

His mind, now a drunken mad monkey, began to hop from one branch to another. It danced a gruesome dance. Showing all its ugly teeth, it teased him. And finally it bit the professor here and there.

Arasu being very sensitive, it took several days to find himself healed when he was just scratched by the monkey. But now it has bitten him. Only his Creator knows whether it will take weeks or months to heal.

A voice that came floating from his back served as a boost and he propped himself up.

"Huh! Hours ago I told you people to throw the dead cat into the dustbin at the street corner. It is still lying there. What obedient children I am blessed with?" said Periyanayaki, the Professor's wife, as she entered the house.

"Oh! You are already here. You look so tired, dear! Wait a minute. I will make lemon tea for you," she said to her husband.

Periyanayaki looked cute in her new yellow-coloured silk sari. A long string of jasmine flowers adorned her pepper and salt tresses woven into a pigtail. A kumkum tilak on her forehead, a platter in her hand carrying a coconut broken into two halves, a few betel leaves, areca nuts, a little string of different flowers and a couple of ripe bananas all spoke to the professor that she was straight from the temple. And to the professor she looked as if the Goddess herself had entered the house to console him.

"Wait a minute," he said to his wife as she was moving into the kitchen. "You said something about a cat. What is it all about?" he asked with curiosity filled eyes.

"Oh! That's a story," said Periyanayaki, "I got ready to participate in the special pooja arranged by the poojari in Gangai Muthu Mariamman temple. When I moved out of the house, I saw a frightened cat running here and there vainly attempting to cross the road. A speeding auto-rickshaw bumped it off and the kitten badly hit was thrown in front of our house. It fell with a thud. It wriggled like a worm on hot sand before it breathed its last. And as I left for the temple, I told our children to throw the dead cat into the bin. I told them two hours ago. And look at the response I had from our children. The carcass should be removed immediately before it could make a mess of itself.

Professor Arasu sat up as the haunting guilt slithered away from him. He felt the sofa seat as soft as ever.

□

Ghost Story

The first ever ghost story I had the thrill of listening to was narrated by my mother. Like many mothers, my mother too was a storyteller… a very good one at that. It is not that that she could not lull me into sleep with her melodious voice that still continues to haunt me even after I have crossed five decades of my sojourn on Earth, but she could keep her listener spell-bound with her gimmicks and also by her special sound effects.

She mimicked the voice of the ferocious wind and the rubbing together of the wings of the cicada. She knew when to be silent. And her silence was as dark as the night itself.

"Years ago when I was a little girl, I saw a ghost. That was the first ghost I ever saw in my life. But it was not the last ghost," began my mother.

"What is a ghost?" I asked as ignorant as ever.

"Listen! Stop asking questions. At the end of the story, you will know what a ghost is. Now listen," she said with a smile.

"In those days of no electricity, hurricane lamps and earthen oil lamps served the purpose of driving away darkness. People who stirred out of their houses in the dark for one reason or the other, invariably carried a hurricane lamp in their hands. They also carried a stick which had a few tiny jingling bells tied to the sides of the stick, so that when they walked, they tapped the ground and the jingling noise of the bells drove creepy crawlies away. If the stick saved them from poisonous insects, the hurricane lamps saved them from falling into ditches, which were plenty on the path. And both the weapons joined hands to dispel ghosts.

"Once I had a stomach disorder, may be because I overate on that day for my mother was an excellent cook. I woke up with a start and felt the urge to ease myself. I didn't dare to wake up anyone in the house for they were all fast asleep.

"I had to cross the backyard of my house, open the bamboo fence gate and then move into the nearby wood, the only place for all the people in the village to deposit night soil. Without making the least noise, I tip-toed my way out with a hurricane lamp.

"The place was so dark that one could not see one's own palm. I had to lift my lamp to dangle it close to my face so as to know my way. The wind was chilled and as I entered the wood, I could hear the music of bamboo plants. The fully grown plants were perhaps hugging and kissing each other and in their wild ecstasy, making eerie sounds. Such a weird sound the wind carried on its wings was enough to make any newcomer take to his heels even in broad daylight. But we were accustomed to all such sounds even in the dead of night. Our way of living demanded it.

"My mother being a highly respected country physician, very good at treating bites, especially dog and snake, took her children along into the wood in search of herbs. This she did only after midnight for she strongly believed that the herbs rejuvenated only after that hour and were able to regain their power lost during sunshine. And we were only lamp bearers to her and she always encouraged her children to turn a deaf ear to all such intimidating sounds for they would only cripple our audacity. Creech… Creech… reech… those were the cicadas. Jal… Jal… Jal… Anybody could easily mistake the sound for tinkling anklets of a woman dancing or running. But we knew that they were sounds made by beetles keen on attracting attention. While such horrendous sounds would easily make many of my playmates dirty their underwears, we were really amazed at the courage we had. Thanks to my mother who instilled courage and hope into us.

And on that night, when I went out to ease myself, the cicadas joined hands with the beetles. Since I knew the musicians of the weird orchestra, no iota of fear gripped my heart.

I sat on my haunches and then, woo… woo… it was the wailing sound of the siren from the nearby cotton mill. I began to wonder what time it was. Was it 3.30 a.m. or 5.00 a.m.? I could think of only those two timings at that odd hour. And I saw someone sitting on his haunches at a stone's throw.

My lamp helplessly watched me screw up my eyes as I tried to decipher who there was. To my great surprise, the man I was trying to have a better look stood up. He was quite tall with only a dhoti on. But for the dhoti, as white as a streak of lightning, he was naked. He had a piece of cloth tied to his head to resemble a turban. God knows whether it was his own loin-cloth, as men used to wear it like that at the early hours when they moved out of their houses to ease themselves.

The man who stood up began to move towards me. For every forward step he took, he grew a foot or so in height.

I couldn't believe my eyes. It was happening as if in a dream with a pinch of magic. Fear gripped me and the next moment I stood up, ready to run for my life. Who can be more dangerous than men to women at such odd hours especially at the loneliness of the wood?

When the tall figure that has grown taller than the tallest palmyra tree in the wood developed swift feet and was just a disastrous distance away, my feet developed wings.

I ran faster than my fastest feet could carry me, though I was not sure whether I could make my escape from the long-footed and long-handed apparition. Yet I didn't lose hope.

My vigilant ears could make out the thud-thud noise of footsteps at my back close at my heels. For the first time, I understood that I was capable of running without my feet touching the ground.

As I ran, I screamed, yelled, wailed and cried. I had almost crossed the wood when I stumped against a root that stood protruding from above the ground and I fell. Before I could raise myself up, I turned back my head to see if I had made my escape. The tallest of the tall ghosts was closing in on me.

My heart thumping louder, I stood up and took to my heels again without even examining whether I was wounded or bleeding from the bruises.

I saw something stretching from behind over my right shoulder. From the corner of my right eye, I saw a long hand trying to overtake me, perhaps to grab me.

I breathed heavily like a terribly tired dog. I did run, of course. In a few seconds, I reached the fence, pushed the wicket gate open and ran into the backyard of my house.

As I entered the backyard, the Sun too rose dispelling darkness. Huffing and puffing, I slumped onto a cane chair inside my house.

My mother who had just finished drawing her usual mammoth kolam in the front yard of the house, made her appearance with a broom in one hand and an empty pitcher in the other.

Seeing my plight, she dropped the pitcher and the broom to the floor and cried: "Eh… eh…eh! What happened?"

With a wave of my hand, I motioned her to wait for a few seconds. She gave me an inquisitive look. I was still gasping for breath. It took quite a long time for me to breathe normal and I saw my mother helplessly watch my plight.

I rehearsed to her from a to z, with bulging eyes and with a frightened face.

On hearing my story with rapt attention my mother, laughed like a shower of granites falling on a hot tin roof.

"Oh! That's only a shit eating ghost. Nothing to fear. It chased you to pull the shit out of you. And you, out of sheer fear, indirectly refused to give the needy ghost what it wanted," she again broke into a guffaw, while I fell to the floor with a thud.

I was told later that I swooned. And no amount of water splashed on my face and later poured on my head ever brought me back to my senses till the temple poojari came home, with a bunch of neem leaves and a pouch full of ash.

The poojari took a fistful of ash, recited mantras and then blew it on to my face. I must have looked like a white apparition. The bunch of neem leaves in his hand in the first round served as a fan on my face but in the second round, metamorphosed itself into a whip. Every blow fell in my face like pinpricks with a sharp slashing sound. It gave me excruciating pain. The leaves that tore away from the bunch fell pell-mell, reminding me of a battlefield full of mutilated bodies of soldiers.

I stood up and made preparations to run away from the scene. But the poojari was all alert and he caught me by my long hair and forced me sit. I began to scream in pain.

"Huh!... Is it that much painful? Then leave this girl and go away this very moment. You don't know how cruel I could be towards spirits like you? Now tell me where are you from? And who are you?" howled the poojari.

"Believe me… I am no spirit. I am a live girl… I am Saguntala… And I am from this house. Don't torture me, please," I pleaded with the poojari.

The merciless poojari raised his voice a few decibels and said: "You are a first rate liar. You better keep away from this little girl or else I know how to pull you out of her body and throw you back into your den. Go away before I do it for you." He then roared at the pitch of his voice, "Quick! Quick… be quick… else you can't even get into your world again. I will nail you to a tree. You will be doomed forever."

I was in a fix. I was not sure what the poojari would do to me.

A few months before, this incident took place. I saw him brand a girl of my age with a red hot iron, all with the purpose of exorcising the evil spirit that was reportedly haunting her. She fell down with a thud and swooned. The poojari took a camphor, ignited it and placed it in the palm of his right hand. He then drew three circles in the air all the time reciting mantras and finally tossed the burning camphor into his wide opened mouth – He leaned back and smiled. Slowly his smile turned into laughter till it became an uproarious one at that. "Ha… Ha… Ha… Ha…"

When everyone was looking askance at the poojari, he howled in a thunderous voice: "I have won you… I have won you. You'll be in my den forever as my slave."

Having witnessed such a scene before, a ruse flashed across my mind. I cried in a loud tone: "Oh, no! oh, no! Don't brand me again with that red hot iron. I can't bear it anymore. You are the cruelest of exorcists I have ever seen in my life. Leave me to myself. I am going… I am gone."

I fell down and swooned. The poojari didn't know that I was pretending; neither did anyone in the crowd enjoying the scene.

"I know… I know who you are. You must be the same spirit that I drove out a few weeks ago." He then finished his preliminaries of lighting camphor, reciting mantras and then gobbling it up. After his customary uproarious laughter, he said in his guttural voice: "I have won you… I have won you again. But this time I'll show no mercy to you. No mercy for the adamant spirit." So saying, he held me by my hair and pulled out as many as he could 'in one go'.

I stomached the pain, woke up with a start and innocently and ignorantly looked for my mother. She came rushing towards me and took me into her ever-loving affectionate hands, and showered kisses on my forehead and cheeks.

"She is quite normal now. You can take her home," said the poojari and blew a handful of ash onto my head and face.

"That was how I made my great escape from the cruel hands of the poojari. In fact, poojaris are crueler than the haunting spirits," said my mother and heaved a sigh.

I was not ready to leave her at that. I became more curious than ever and asked: "What would the poojari do with the strand of hair he had pulled out of my head?"

"Oh, that! That he would take to the nearby palmyra tree with no companions. He would have the strand of hair nailed into the tree. By doing such a thing, he made us believe that he had saved us from an impending disaster. For all such acts of exorcism, he charged a cockerel and a big fat hen. Above all, we had to pay him 4 annas.

Years later, when I rehearsed my mother's experience with a ghost and a poojari to my uncle Samarapuri, he came out with his weird experience with a ghost.

Samarapuri was dark-complexioned, short-statured but well-built. He was not visible in the dark unless the moon, particularly chose him to shower her cool rays. He himself would easily pass for an apparition in the midst of people who see him for the first time. Most often he was seen with his clean white dhoti kilted up and he hated to put on any shirt. He had a white towel which went round his hip when he was at work in the paddy field. The very same towel covered his torso when he moved around the village on business errands. And the same towel became his headgear when he sat on branches of trees eating their fruits, already tasted and abandoned by squirrels.

He spent the nights on the big broad pyal of my grandma's palatial house. Adjacent to the house ran a lane that led to the wood, the very same wood my mother had bitter experiences with the shit-eating ghost.

Samarapuri was asleep when he heard someone call him by his name. The voice sounded as though it came from the other world and he cared a hair for it. The voice sounded again and this time it was louder than before. When he realized that the call was from his father, he woke up with a start.

He sat up. He saw his father standing on the muddy road. He squeezed his eyelids and looked at his father again.

"Hei! Come on…Light up that lantern by your side and bring it along," said his father.

"Where are we going, pa?" It was the innocent Samarapuri.

"I feel uneasy in the stomach. I need to go to the woods to ease myself. Give me company. Bring with you the burning lantern," said his father.

Samarapuri looked around. The parading Moon was quite bright, trying its best to show everything in its proper shape and colour as the sun would during his duty hours. "The moon is so bright… Why do you need me at this hour?" asked the impertinent Samarapuri.

His father didn't answer.

"Who can be a better companion than the Moon? Pa! On many occasions like this when I asked for your company, you gave me the lantern and advised me not to be afraid of the dark and face the world as a man should… And now you need my company eh! Ha! Ha! Ha! What a funny world? Ha! Ha! Ha!" Samarapuri laughed. His father too, as if he wanted to digest his son's dig, laughed uproariously.

"Hei! Come on…This is no time for joke…Bring the lantern along," he said and moved away quite fast.

Samarapuri simply obeyed. He took the lantern and raised the wick a little up so that there could be more light and began walking behind his father nurturing no grudge.

Poor Samarapuri couldn't cope with his father's speed as his steps were quite long and fast. In fact, he was fleeing. Samarapuri was almost running after his father with the lantern dangling from his left hand.

"Why is he moving so fast?" Samarapuri asked himself. "He must be really sick," he answered his own question. Seconds later, he thought why that old man was not stopping to ease himself. His father was not of that type to shy away from human presence or hide behind trees to answer nature calls. He never even bothered about the presence of women, when his bladder declared emergency. Why should such a man go farther and farther into the wood and that too at dead of night? Was he afraid of the moon playing 'hide and seek' amidst the fluffy cotton bale-like clouds?

The cicadas all of a sudden began to chirp and a stray owl on wings let out two blood-curdling hoots. The frogs began to crock and sent jitters down my spine. "I was scared of croaking frogs because those ignoramuses did not in the least know that they were inviting trouble. Their croaking is simply a dining bell for snakes. And when snakes rush for their food, they do not spare the human trespassers," sermonized Samarapuri.

Oh! Is that the reason why Samarapuri's father was moving with such long and fast steps?

Samarapuri had the shock of his life when he saw his father cross a well without any effort.

A well in the wood! Surprising indeed! No one knew when the well was dug and for what reason! During rainy days, rain water found its way into the well and filled the huge well. Since it had a ground level mouth, many stepped into it unaware of its existence. They never came back alive to tell any story about it. But people concocted several stories about the well with the spirits and the goblins that were haunting it.

Samarapuri was shocked to his coccyx bone because no human being would ever be able to cross that huge mouthed well without falling into it. Stunned he stood, this time gazing at his father's amazing activity. But his father was going ahead, without even turning his head once to see if his son was following him or not.

How did his father cross that wide-mouthed huge well with little or no effort when no one else escaped from its mouth?

The very thought was enough to make him freeze. And he froze.

As Samarapuri finished narrating his story, I was still in a fix for I was not sure what he saw and what was it that made him freeze.

I gave him an inquiring look. Samarapuri read my curiosity-filled eyes. He wound up the tale by saying: I froze because I realized that my father died long ago when I was still in my teens.

It was time for me to freeze.

□

Nirvana

"Be careful of your speech. Don't talk too much for talk leads to calamity," wrote Confucius on a wall inside his house. He read and re-read the sentence and heaved a sigh. He found it difficult to recover from the shock his enemies gave.

Largely self-educated, he was proud of the several positions he held in the state of Lu, in China. A school teacher for a start, he rose to the level of minister of Justice. That was the highest honour a commoner could dream of. But he felt too restless to stop teaching, a profession he always loved. Wherever he was, he busied himself and many preferred to stay away from his loud-mouthed teaching.

"What harm will come to Confucius if he rests his tongue a few days?" asked a few.

"The more he mixes in company, the more he becomes loquacious," said others and shunned his presence.

How can a teacher, who loved his art, ever hold his tongue? Confucius asked himself as he stood morosely at the threshold of his house, his face pinched by grief. Having decided to leave his 'enemies', as he called all those who run away at his very sight, to the solitude they preferred, he moved out giving a free rein to his sturdy legs.

He was not sure how many miles his legs have carried him but he was sure he was quite far from his home, when he came across some boys playing in the paddy field. He looked around and saw one boy sitting alone on a nearby mound, his back against the trunk of an age-old saal tree.

Confucius moved towards that lonely boy, bent down and leaned forward.

The boy looked at the elderly person, dressed in a silk tunic with a couple of golden rings prominent on his fingers.

Confucius smiled at him and asked, "Do you know who I am?"

"What does it matter to me?" retorted the lonely boy. "Leave me alone. I am working." He looked down at the ground as though reflecting on something.

The boy's reply was a blow to his ego he had cherished all these years. He knew he should say something to the lonely boy but couldn't find words.

Confucius was not sure what to say. So he mumbled, "A time to work and a time to play. When your friends are playing over there, why are you working?"

The boy looked at him squarely. He then said, "They were working when I was playing. Shouldn't I work when they play?"

His words pattered like a distant rain shower around Confucius. The teacher in him was not ready to leave the boy at that. He had to say something. He heard himself saying, "I am a teacher." There was nothing else he could say. "I am a teacher," he repeated.

"I hate them," retorted the boy without even looking at the teacher.

"No, no, no." Confucius sat with a thud facing the boy. "Imagine a world without teachers. You boys have to rot in ignorance."

"Ludicrous," said the boy. After a prolonged stare, he said, "Who can be a better teacher than Nature herself? You teachers always underestimate your students. Always meddling, meddling and meddling. You ask this, you ask that and you are always dissatisfied with their answers… You are always ready to offer all kinds of advice as though the youngsters could not function without you."

Confucius turned his head to see what the other boys were doing. They were playing 'hide and seek'. Their voices hummed, buzzed, erupted in laughter and vanished into hushes. "I have to tell you people what I think. Otherwise this world will eat you raw."

The lonely boy let out a long, but decent, chuckle. "You are so spoilt by your students, dear sir, you act like a king."

With an acrimony, he could not help, Confucius asked, "If you think you learn from Nature, tell me what fire has no smoke, what water no fish, what hill no stones, what tree no branches?"

The boy, without a moment's hesitation, said, "A glow-worm's fire has no smoke, well water no fish, a mound of earth no stones and a rotten tree no branches."

Pleased with the thoughts of the boy, Confucius went ahead. "What is in Nature that has not enough and what has a surplus?"

The boy in one effortless move tossed the answer, "A winter's day is not long enough and a summer's day is too long."

Confucius asked again, "Do you know what are the connecting bonds between Heaven and Earth? Who is husband and who is wife?"

"Yes," said the boy, "Heaven is Father and Earth is Mother. The sun is husband and the moon wife."

"And which do you say is the closer relationship, father and mother or husband and wife?"

"One's parents are close; husband and wife are not so close."

Confucius guffawed before he said, "How can you say they are not closely related? Don't you know that husband and wife sleep under the same coverlet while alive and lie in the same grave when dead?"

"Let this be your last question… I told you I am at work observing two ants playing near my feet. I am sure you have not noticed them. Now to my answer… A man without a wife is like a cart without a wheel. But it is easy to get a new wheel. Likewise, if a wife dies, her husband goes for a new one… Three windows and six lattices do not give the light admitted by one door. Can all the stars in the sky with their sparkling brilliance ever equal the splendour of the solitary moon? So is it with the affection of a father and mother. It is unique, dear teacher, and alas, if it be lost."

Confucius nodded his head in approval. Before he could go on, the boy said, "Thanks to Nature, my teacher. Will you give me the answers I am in search of for certain questions?"

Before Confucius could respond, the boy shot a volley of questions, "Why is it that mallards and ducks are able to swim? How is it that wild geese and cranes can sing? Why are firs and pine-trees green throughout the winter?"

The moment was unexpected as were the questions. A flash of animosity flared up in Confucius. Yet he tried, "Ducks and mallards can swim because they are blessed with broad feet. Wild geese and cranes can sing because they have long necks. Firs and pine-trees continue to be green through the winter because they have strong hearts."

The boy remarked coldly, "Fishes and turtles too swim… do they have broad feet? Frogs and toads too can sing… Are they long-necked? The bamboo too maintains its freshness in winter… Is it because of its strong heart?"

After a short pause, the boy asked, "Tell me at least this… How many stars are there altogether in the sky?"

"We are not competent enough to talk about the sky," said Confucius, a bit scared of the boy. "Ask me something about the earth."

"Then tell me how many houses are there on the earth," the boy demanded.

"Can't you ask about something that is before our eyes… why must you ask about heaven and earth?" the teacher asked and bit his tongue.

"Ha! Ha! Ha! You want me to ask about something that is before our eyes. Well! Well! How many hairs are there in your eyebrows?"

Confucius' head ached and his eyes smarted. His limbs felt bloated and insensate, and a sour taste coated his tongue.

The boy continued, "You are proud to be a teacher but you have not learnt much. Every good teacher should first of all be a learner. Everyday I learn… all self-education. Now go on your way and do not return till you find answers to my questions. And if at all you return, do not teach."

Then, without a word, the boy rose and left the mound to join the other boys at play.

Confucius shot him a terrorized look. He felt suddenly unburdened. Now completely unshackled, he tried to live in a future freed of meaning.

□

Penalty

"This story is as old as the world," said the storyteller, lifting a mug of toddy up to his parched dark lips. He ran his tongue on the lips in an attempt to wet them. "And this toddy is as old as the Gods themselves," he said, placing the emptied mug in front of him on a small heap of sand. "Let your tribe increase," he said after a belch.

He picked up a live cheroot that was idling on the sand-heap, took a drag out of it, and returned it thoughtfully. Smoke gushed forth from his mouth as it would from a steam engine.

"Only one story for one mug of toddy," said the old man with a broad smile.

"O.K. But don't sleep off your hangover before you complete the story," warned the collector of tales.

The old man laughed. "One mug of toddy can't rock me to sleep. It can only inspire me," he said and added after a pause, "But promise me that you will come again with a mug of toddy tomorrow – for another tale, of course".

"Yes. I'll be here to spend my evenings with you till you go bankrupt of tales."

"Let us see who goes bankrupt," said the storyteller with a sly smile. "Today is *Ammavasai*, New Moon day. The moon has put on his pitch-dark garment and gone into mourning."

"Oh, has he?" the collector of tales asked and became jubilant, "But over what?"

"Therein lies a tale," said the old man. He let out the last puff of his cheroot, and discarded the stub. He pressed his right forefinger and middle finger against his lips and sent a jet of white dribble from his mouth flying across like a dart.

The tale-collector's cassette recorder was on. The old man began to tell the story:

Several centuries ago, only the moon knows when lived an unhappy couple. They were unhappy because they had no child to call their own.

The husband, of course, was an understanding and gentle fellow. Never did he show a hard face to her, nor used a harsh word against her over her barrenness. But since every other couple in the village was blessed with a brood of children, they found delight in teasing and insulting the childless woman. Whenever she happened to pass by, they spat on the floor and treated her very presence as a bad omen. They never allowed their children to go anywhere near her for they believed that a barren woman is a cursed creature, destined to spread her evil spell on the children. Beggars too didn't take alms from her for they feared that if they took anything from her hands, they would have a tough time for the rest of their lives and their begging bowls too would go barren.

The childless woman wept over her fate. There was not a single temple that she did not visit to offer her oblations and there was not a single God to whom she didn't pray. But no god listened to her prayer.

Since everyone in the village hated her, she stopped going out of her house. Her husband and her widowed mother-in-law were her only human contacts.

After some time, the mother-in-law too began to show signs of hatred. Once she complained: "What a woman I have brought to my house for my son! A cock too may lay eggs. But never will this wench give birth to a babe... Never. Is my son destined to be the last in the long list of the great lineage?"

The daughter-in-law, unable to hold herself, cried and wept. The husband turned a deaf ear to her cries, which only indicated that he didn't disagree with his mother's words.

One day she overheard her mother-in-law brainwashing her son to marry some other girl of his choice who would bring forth children.

At first, the husband was reluctant. But since his mother insisted that he should opt for a second marriage in order to leave a copy of himself in this world, he agreed.

The childless woman cursed her fate. As a protest against the decision taken by her husband, she began to live in the backyard of the house. She spent most of her time with tear-flooded eyes raised heavenward.

Meanwhile, the mother-in-law busied herself consulting astrologers in order to select a fertile woman for her son.

The husband, though for want of progeny nodded to his mother's wishes, didn't in the least develop any sort of hatred for his wife. He pleaded with her to come back home. But she didn't budge. Amidst her tears, she said: "It's enough if you allow me to live here in the backyard of your house. The cowshed is the right place for a barren woman like me to live in. Let your would-be, who is supposed to be fertile, occupy the house. Two wives of the same husband can't live under one roof."

Though all the attempts of the husband to bring his wife back home fizzled out, he didn't fail in his duties as a husband. He saw to it that she was regularly fed.

Days passed. On one full-moon night, she sat in the open air with her silver plate containing sauce-mixed rice. She was not hungry enough to eat. Hence, she went on looking at the glorious moon. Within seconds, she forgot herself and all her gnawing worries. She imagined that there sat a lovely child on the moon with all smiles. It opened its wee mouth as if it were eager to take food from her hands.

The woman quickly rolled a handful of rice into a ball and raised her hand affectionately towards the child.

The Moon-God who was hurrying homeward in his chariot looked down by sheer accident. He saw a woman offering him food. What attracted him more towards her was the untold affection and love with which she offered it.

He called a sudden halt to his chariot, got down and began to move towards the woman.

The woman who had been so far in a reverie was startled to see the Moon-God himself coming towards her. Spellbound she stood and the Moon-God took food from her affectionate hands.

The silver plate became empty, and the Moon-God belched with satisfaction. "*Amma*!" (mother) he called. His eyes were filled with gratitude.

Words would fail to convey the joy she experienced at the uttering of the word *Amma*!

Hot tears began to trickle out of her eyes. The Moon-God stood dumbstruck at the sight of the woman in tears.

"*Amma!*" He called again. "You have given me food mixed with affection and love. And now I do not understand the meaning of your tears. If you have any unfulfilled *aasai* (desire), please tell me. I will try to fulfill it."

The barren woman continued to weep in silence. The Moon-God too stood silent all the time expecting a reply.

Minutes later the woman opened her mouth. "Lord! You have called me *Amma*. I don't have a child to call me so. And my *aasai* is to have one."

The Moon-God smiled and said: "You have showed me love and affection. It is my duty to fulfill your desire… You will have a son."

The woman prostrated herself before the Moon-God and washed his feet with tears of gratitude.

A few days later, the woman's body began to show signs of pregnancy. The husband jumped for joy and the mother-in-law stopped visiting astrologers. The neighbours too began to be friendly with her.

Every night she waited in the backyard of her house with a plate full of sauce-mixed rice. The Moon-God came without fail and took food from her affectionate and loving hands.

Years passed. The blessed child grew to be a young man. And the Moon-God never disappointed the woman by absenting himself on any of the nights.

One day the woman passed away due to the ailments of old age. Before she breathed her last, she told her son to offer food to the moon on her behalf every night. Her son agreed.

On the night of the woman's death, the Moon-God came only to find the woman's son waiting in the backyard.

"Where is your mother?" asked the Moon-God.

"She is dead. I'm here to serve you food," the son replied trembling with fear. It was for the first time he was listening to a heavenly voice.

The Moon-God was disappointed. Tears collected in his eyes and threatened to trickle down. He wiped his tears and said: "I have never before seen such an affectionate mother. Oh! How I wish her to be alive to offer me food with the same sort of love. But now that she is gone, I'll mourn over her death once a month."

That is the reason why the Moon-God wears a pitch-dark garment and goes into mourning over the death of the *amma* whose *aasai* he has fulfilled. The night the moon shuts himself in his abode is known in Tamil as *Ammavasai* (the New Moon). This is also the reason why the living sons of dead mothers offer food to the Moon-God on the night when he goes into mourning.

The old storyteller pulled a cheroot from somewhere under his turban and lighted it.

"Quite interesting," remarked the tale-collector.

"I have more interesting tales to tell you. If you come a little early tomorrow evening, I may tell you a longer one. I will narrate how the sun and the moon were uterine brothers, and why their mother cursed the sun and blessed the moon."

"Oh sure. Certainly I will come with a mug of toddy for you."

"Good! Keep your words," the old man said and added lustfully, "A fillet of fried fish is also welcome."

The storyteller reclined with his back to the mud wall of his hut and rolled his towel into a ball to rest his head. "This is worth more than everything else," he murmured.

□

Sri Aurobindo's Shoes

By five in the evening, the tired Pondicherry sun rushes home, as would a policeman after his duty hours. To the locals it is a feast for the eyes and to the outsiders a sight to dream of.

All roads here lead to the Bay of Bengal. Once near the sea, the promenade lures us to take a long walk from North to South and then the temptation of strolling from South to North crops up. The chill cool evening sea breeze hugs and fans us with its invisible wings and we feel as if we were graced and kissed by the hem of a silk-soft sari that adorns a beauty.

This promenade has a story to tell. The British were always a threat to the French. The French considered the British as a synonym for 'tsunami'. To prevent their attack from the sea, the French in Pondicherry constructed a long wall on the shore. We can sit on it, walk on it hand in hand with a friend, dance on it, even stretch ourselves and sleep on it. Aren't we helpless in the hands of the breeze, once it lulls us into sleep? What a pleasant feeling our mind and body experience at the very thought of it?

Sundal, murukku, elladai, all goodies announce their arrival hiding inside a bamboo basket conveniently seated on the shoulders of hawkers.

Sundal, a mixture of baked peas with tiny slivers of mango and ginger added with grated coconut soon finds shelter in the stomachs of the beach goers and allows the empty baskets to go home. But *murukku* and *elladai,* not soft as *sundal* and sometimes hard for the teeth, have to raise their voice a few decibels more. By the time their voice subsides, multi-coloured ice-shavings on sticks, sweet ice-cubes start hawking themselves.

People throng the seashore to enjoy the breeze free of cost and join their friends to munch the goodies and chit-chat with them for hours together.

To that seashore, two men with their dangling tufts of hair were found walking, all the time swinging their hands to synchronize with their fast legs. They were passing through Kalathi Eswaran Temple Street. As they progressed, Manakula Vinayagar Temple street criss-crossed them. They halted awhile, turned to their right, crossed their hands against their chests and held their earlobes with their pointing fingers and thumbs, squatted down and rose again a number of times, then rapped their temples softly before they resumed their walk.

Rue Francois Martin crossed their path. As they were walking very fast, it soon faded from their view. The next street named after a saint, Rue Saint Louis crossed. Then there is only one more street – Rue de la Compagne. No other street would cross their path and they would find themselves on the seashore, to be given a hearty welcome by the breeze with a hug.

When they were about to cross Rue Saint Louis, one of the two walkers as if by a reflex action turned his head to his left. "Hei! Look…look…a crowd has collected there. What's up?" asked he.

The other replied, "Yes! Yes! That's Ragava Chettiar's house. Three fellows are standing in the street talking earnestly. But how can you call it a crowd? Oh, no! Three do not make a crowd."

"If that is not a crowd, then what else? Look who is addressing the others! He is Bharati. That man in a black coat and a strange headgear. Watch what he does. He finds pleasure in twirling up his moustaches while he speaks.

He is a one-man army. Is not an army a crowd of soldiers? Madcap! Madcap!" lectured the first.

"Madcap?" retorted the second. "You call Bharati a madcap, eh? What nonsense are you talking? I have heard people praise him sky high. He is known by several titles. Some call him a *siddha purusha*. Some call him a yogi and philosopher. Everybody calls him a great poet. But you… you are indifferent towards Bharati."

"No…no…everyone in Pondicherry calls him a madcap. Come, let us go there and find out why they are all standing there." They continued with their conversation as they turned and entered Rue Saint Louis and moved towards Ragava Chettiar's house. It bore the door number 13.

The man who thought Bharati a madcap, went close to Bharati and asked, "what ho, Bharati! What is this crowd for? Anyone died in Chettiar's house?"

Bharati stopped twirling his moustaches awhile and looked daggers at him. "Hei! You belong to the lots that rush to the seashore, eat goodies sold there, chat with friends and practise mudslinging as an art. Go… go away before somebody else walks away with the breeze due to you. Go away," roared Bharati, his eyes fuming.

"Cool down, Bharati. I only wanted to know why you people are all standing here. That's all."

"Why do you want to know?" howled Bharati, "Even if I tell you, it won't get into your thick head. Don't you know that Sri Aurobindo lives in this house? Chettiar has rented it out to him. Right now he is meditating. When he finishes, we will join him for a conversation that will touch on art, literature, spirituality and national politics. Then we will part. We are waiting for him to finish. Enough? Or you want to know more?" Bharati giggled. His friends looked as if they were about to burst into laughter.

Ashamed, the two walkers stood staring at Bharati. They felt as if they had had a very long illness, and had only just begun to recover.

"Enough Bharati! Enough...My head has already started reeling. Nothing has gone into my head. You go and while away your time talking all blah blah. Madcaps make friends only with other madcaps," so saying they began to move.

Bharati laughed like a shower of granites falling on a hot tin roof. That called a halt to their legs.

"You need at least a small quantity of brain to understand what I said. I know you are empty-skulled. Sri Aurobindo too in a letter informed his wife Mrinalini of his three madnesses that keep him in their grip. Without having the faintest idea, you called us all madcaps. We are happy about it. But don't you know what madcaps are capable of? Before we do it on you, run for your life."

Bharati sounded defensive; he couldn't help it. As he gritted his teeth, the helpless two took to their heels with hurt pride.

A bit over-excited, his friends smiled. Bharati smiled back and said, "We should give these fellows in their own coin."

"Bharati!" A call came from the inner courtyard of the house and attracted the attention of Bharati and his friends. They turned to see the thin frame of a man, light enough to be carried away by even a calm breeze, emerging from the house. A jasmine-white towel adorned his torso and a milk-white dhoti covered his trunk. His head looked as if it had not met a barber for more than a year.

"That's Nolini. His presence is a bell to us. That is to say Sri Aurobindo has finished his meditation and that he is expecting us. Come, let us get inside and seek the blessings of Sri Aurobindo, Goddess Saraswati incarnate." Bharati's words pleased the others enormously and they thought the second part of the message had proved important after all.

Bharati joined his hands to his back, and with his chest up, entered the house as a lion would with pride-filled eyes. His friends V.V.S. Iyer and Mandayam Srinivasachari unable to cope with his speed dutifully ran after him.

"Ha, Ghosh! Holding your shoes in your hands? What are you upto? Your actions always seem different to me." Bharati's voice entered first before his frame could.

"Ho, Ba! Come, come. Welcome friends. Come in. Feel comfortable," Sri Aurobindo said, pointing his hand to the floor. They all sat on the floor and found themselves in the company of Nolini and a few other well-wishers of the Mahayogi.

Combing his beard with his fingers, Sri Aurobindo smiled and said, "A few days ago, this pair of leather shoes reached me from Calcutta. My younger brother, Barin, has sent them. I was applying coconut oil on their inner edges, all to stop them from pinching my feet."

Bharati heaved a sigh. "No knife, however sharp, can even slash the one endowed with a younger brother. Our wise men had said so long ago. How true are these words! You are blessed with a younger brother, my dear Ghosh, to fulfill all your demands. But who is there for me to send me a pair of shoes for the asking?"

Sri Aurobindo smiled through his eyes before he started off the conversation on shoes. Who of our first parents would have invented shoes and with what raw material were they made? Who at a later date fashioned them? When workers in shoe manufacturing firms of Japan wish to go on a strike, how do they go on? Several such questions were asked in that evening talks with Sri Aurobindo. The Uttara Yogi went on answering them supporting his views with pages from the past.

The session was fun, filled with laughter. Sri Aurobindo wound up the session by saying, "Humour is the salt of existence."

Bharati reached for Sri Aurobindo's shoes, and took them very awkwardly and sat looking at them, as if he didn't quite know what to do next.

It was time for them to part. How fast time flies when like-minded people open their hearts and minds! When they moved out of the house and stepped on the street, their faces looked illumined as if they had tasted nectar from the Heavens.

"The greatness of Sri Aurobindo rests in his sound knowledge and deep understanding of life. How beautifully he was harping on the origin and growth of shoes. Surely he is a being to be wondered at. Bharati! As you have said, Sri Aurobindo is the very incarnation of Goddess of Knowledge," commended V.V.S. Iyer graciously.

"Who can doubt it? Ghosh is a male counterpart of Goddess Saraswati. She always blesses us with her boons," so saying Bharati looked down admiring his feet. A mischievous smile lingered on his face.

Sri Aurobindo's eyes ransacked the whole room for his shoes. Seconds later, he smiled a broad smile, and sat before his writing desk. His pen began to move on a sheet of paper.

Dear Barin,

Send me a pair of shoes as early as you can. My Tamil friend Ba has walked away with the ones you had sent me. In fact, his need is greater than mine, for his legs carry him to every nook and cranny of Pondicherry. You are there always ready to buy for me whatever I ask of you. But poor Ba! He has none.

He signed…Sri Aurobindo Ghosh. Once again, he smiled through his eyes.

□

The Fun Lover

On a sultry afternoon, when all my family members left for a nearby temple to participate in the fun and fanfare of the festivities there, I was left alone in my house with my toddler grandson.

Like me, my grandson has taken a liking neither for the temple nor for the stone gods installed there. Neither his mother nor his grandmother, to whom he was very much attached, could ever cajole him into visiting places of worship.

For a long time, my son too strictly followed my ideals and shunned from going to temples. God knows what really happened…a dramatic change took place after his marriage. He stopped loitering around and began visiting places of worship with his wife.

I am like my father and no amount of advice from my pious better half had ever helped me in changing my views about temples and stone gods. Only the Lord in the firmament knows when my grandson would abandon his grandpa's ideals and stick to his grandma's.

Before I start this story, I must introduce the hero to you. He is the very same fellow, left under my care in the loneliness of the house. I registered his name as Ramana when he was born in a private hospital, though very rarely others call him by that name. He has several names to his credit, all of them coined by the witnesses of his mischief. And he himself, perhaps confused with the different names he was called by, would give different names at different times when he was asked: "What is your name, child?"

Ramana's favourites are cell phones. Almost everyone in my family has one or two cell phones to call his or her own. The child is quite familiar with all the brand names of our cell phones and so he would answer "My name is Nokia," other times he would say, "I am Samsung," sometimes he would club two brand names and coin one on his own, and say, "My name is LG Motorola" or Blackberry Lava," thereby putting everyone to peals of laughter.

Ramana knows not only the several brand names of cells but also the ways of handling them. At times, he would send empty messages to friends, who will call back to know what that empty message was meant for. He would press buttons of his choice and call people. And when he hears a response from the other aside, he would either howl into the machine and put the one at the receiving end to fright or sing the nursery rhymes he had learnt by heart and give a concert to the listener and carry him to dizzy heights. Sometimes, he would simply keep mum and drive the listener to the verge of madness. After a while, he would put it into the refrigerator and run away to play.

Those who accidentally see the cell in that unwanted place would rush to its rescue, smiling at the mischief of the child. "Thank god, the freezer is too high for him to reach," they would mumble and hand it over to its owner.

The double-door refrigerator served as a 'safe' for Ramana, and he kept only the valuables there. Sometimes we came across his playthings, like tiny cars, spinning tops, half-chewed chocolates, etc. Wc rarcly disturbed them for we were happy to know that the child was learning the value of things.

Once when I was in a hurry to go out to keep an appointment with a writer, someone handed over my house tax bill and said that the tax should be paid within fifteen days from the date mentioned. I handed it over to my wife, standing at the gate to see me off and said, "Keep it safe."

Ramana seated on my wife's hip – that was the seat he highly preferred for where could he find such a cozy seat – perhaps understood the value of the demand from the government.

A week or so later, when I asked for the bill, my wife became panicky for she forgot its whereabouts. A bickering ensued and a little later, Ramana prattled, "Hai! Hai!" perhaps with the intention of putting an end to our quarrel and dragged his grandma to the refrigerator. He then opened the bottom door and told her to pull out the vegetable container at the bottom tray.

We were all smiles when we saw the house tax bill resting there. But poor thing! It got completely soaked. With great care, we took it out and dried it up in the sun. Thank god, we got the bill but the details of the amount to be paid were smudged and hard to decipher.

How I was looked down upon and jeered at by the cashier in the Municipality would make another interesting story. But I would better stop here and go ahead with the story I want to tell you.

Stretching myself and relaxing in the sofa, I was watching my favourite Animal Planet channel. Ramana was resting his head in the crook of my arm, his wee body close to my chest and his one leg on my tummy; he was meddling with my Blackberry, a present from my second son settled in Canada.

After a while, Ramana fed up with the digital game he was playing, gave the machine to me and said that he wanted to listen to music and songs. I switched on the FM radio and handed it over to him in order to keep him cool and away from his monkey business.

A half hour would have passed. I was engrossed in the life and style of Amazon women they were showing on the channel. Ramana was deep asleep. I released the Blackberry from his sleeping hands and switched off the radio.

I do not know when I dozed off. Is sleep contagious? I was startled out of sleep, when my landline screamed.

I rushed to know who the caller was.

The moment I said 'hello' into the receiver, I heard my wife banging me from the other end.

"How many times did I call you over your cell? Where the hell have you disappeared? Is Ramana alright? Is he troubling you? I don't think that we will be able to reach home before dark. The temple is overcrowded and we have not yet seen the Lord. To wriggle our way out through this milling crowd would be far from easy. Feed the child if he complains of hunger. All that you have to do is to boil the milk kept on the oven. Don't forget to add a little sugar. Give him biscuits if he asks. Biscuits are in the tin kept in the kitchen cupboard. If you have to go out, take Ramana along with you. Don't forget to handover the door key to that talkative old lady in the opposite house. Don't forget to take your cell phone with you, when you go out."

I heaved a sigh of relief, when she disconnected her cell phone.

My eyes began to search for my Blackberry. I couldn't find it anywhere. And the sleeping child was also missing.

"Where the hell has this child gone along with my cell phone?" I asked myself and called out his name.

There was absolutely no response. I entered one room after another. He was not to be seen anywhere. Neither was my Blackberry.

I began to bellow out his name Ramana…Ramana… Ramana…There was no response.

I was sure that the fellow had not moved out of the house for the main door remained bolted. I rushed to the backyard of the house, entered the loo and then the bathroom. He was not found anywhere there.

Something in me said that he was involved in a bigger mischief, for he was a shrewd organizer of such things. The only place I had not yet searched for him was my study.

Yes! Ramana was there. I found him preoccupied with a big fat book. "Hei! What are you doing here?" I asked.

He smiled and said, "I am busy. Don't disturb." He simply aped what I used to tell him when he entered my study.

As I went nearer to him, I found that he had already pulled out a few pages of a dictionary and had torn them to shreds.

Wild with rage, I pulled out the dictionary from him, only to find out that all the pages under 'A' had gone and that he had started tearing the pages under 'B'.

There was no use in howling at the child. For if he began to howl back, nothing on earth could stop him.

"You shouldn't have done this," I said to him showing the shreds that covered the floor, all the time maintaining my unusual calm.

Ramana continued with the work and said, "Don't disturb. I am busy."

I had no other option but to okay his work. I had lost several books from my library to rats, squirrels and moths. So. why not a few to a lovable biped?

"When will you be free, Sir?" I asked in all humility, with my arms across my chest and my body bent forward.

"Why?" Ramana asked, without even taking away his eyes from the book he was butchering.

I said, "Sir! I need my cell phone. Where have you kept it? Give it back to me and I will leave you to your serious work."

"Oh! Your Blackberry? It's safe thatha," said he.

The word 'safe' reminded me of Ramana's safest world – the refrigerator. From my study, I shuffled my way to the kitchen. I opened the big door and then the small one above…ransacked the whole machine. But there was no trace of my poor Blackberry.

I made my hunt for my Blackberry in all the favourite haunts of Ramana in the house. It was nowhere to be found.

My creative brain hit upon an idea. Why should not I try to wake up my slumbering Blackberry through my landline? Immediately, I dialled my cell number. For a few seconds, there was only a beep…beep…beep response… And then a mellifluous voice said, "The cell phone number you are trying to reach is currently switched off."

My God! Now the job of finding my cell phone has become all the more difficult. And the only one rescuer I could think of was Ramana.

I rushed back to my study. Ramana was busily engaged in shredding every page of the dictionary. My writing desk and the floor were cluttered with the broken parts of many of my pens that adorned the desk. Many of them do not write and that is another story; all the handiwork of Ramana.

"Ramana, dear! Where is my cell phone?" I cooed.

"Ramana gave an innocent look and then continued with his work. Perhaps he thought why this old man wanted to get the answer again, when he had already given it.

"Ramana, my little darling! Where did you put my cell phone? Blackberry! Blackberry?"

"Blackberry is safe thatha." He said without even shifting his eyes from the mutilated dictionary."

"Yes, my child! I know Blackberry is safe. But where did you keep it? It is not there in the refrigerator. And I can't find it anywhere. Will you please help? I have to give a call to someone very urgently."

"Who is it, thatha?" Ramana asked.

"You do not know him. Please help," I held his chin and coaxed him.

Ramana shook his head as if he wanted to say he would not budge from the place, since I was going to give a call to someone he was not familiar with.

"Come on, Ramana! Please, please," I said and showered his face with kisses.

Ramana smiled and said, "I will show you where it is, provided you help me in tearing this book."

"Sure! Sure! I will give you another fat book to tear. But now help me out in getting my Blackberry," I pleaded.

Ramana again shook his head and said, "Only after finishing my work."

I had no other way but to help him in tearing the dictionary. It took another half hour to tear page after page and then shred it.

The work was over. That was what I thought. But Ramana gave me the hard cover of the dictionary and, motioned me to tear it. I put all my strength to action and with great difficulty, managed to tear the hardboard into several bits.

Ramana clapped his hands in appreciation of my muscle power put to proper use. He let out a guffaw. I knew its meaning: "Rats too would not have done such a clean job of it."

He then held my hand and dragged me to the kitchen.

"It's not there in the refrigerator!" I said.

"Yes! It's not there...I know where it is... It's safe," so saying, he dragged me further and stood near the kitchen sink. "Here," he said.

"Where?" I asked with all curiosity.

"Here... inside this," he said pointing at a big bucket of dirty water.

My heart began to beat faster than ever.

"Is my Blackberry in this bucket of swill?" I asked.

"Yes, thatha! The Blackberry stopped singing songs to me. And so I punished it by throwing it into this bucket."

I titled the bucket to its left and emptied it. The little fellow, with his arms akimbo, was looking at the flowing dirty water.

"Ah! There it is," he cried, "Ah! There it is… I told you, you know, it is safe," Ramana said in glee.

Yes! My blackberry was safe, drenched to its sim. Without losing a second, I pulled my Blackberry out, shook off the dirty water….

"Why did you do this?" I howled at Ramana. The animal in me came up.

"It stopped singing me songs. It became useless," he said, his eyes brimming with fear.

I remember to have told him that all useless things should go into the bucket. I never knew that he would follow every syllable of my advice.

The animal in me looked daggers at the child.

"Thatha," Ramana called, expressing genuine fear. "Will you give me the second big fat book?" he asked.

"What for?" I asked gritting my teeth.

"To tear," said the child laughing at the ugliness of my face.

The animal in me disappeared and the god came up.

□

The Tooth

That night thoughts about my dead father rushed and pitched their tent. Thoughts are very hard, cruel beings. They look like the very incarnation of angels from the nether world and they badger us for hours together, sometimes for days. They speak and laugh with guttural voices. They make such coarse music that sleep slithers away from us and take to its viewless wings.

This is what sleep is capable of when thoughts invade in battalions. That night sleep left me in the lurch.

On such occasions, I rarely curse sleep. I treat it as a blessing and straightaway go to my father's almirah made of Burma teak, open it and pull out one of the diaries my father used to jot down the special happenings in his life.

Dead man tells no tales, they say. Nevertheless, the diaries kept by my father tell many tales about him.

I pulled out one from the rows and rows of diaries. I must hasten to tell that my father meticulously kept his diaries until he lapsed into a coma. He died at the ripe old age of 87. I rarely disturb his almirah and maintain it as a little family museum. And so, even if my father comes back on a dashing visit from that undiscovered country from whose bourn no traveller returns, he would see the contents of his almirah intact, as he had left them some twenty years back.

I took the diary to my bed, switched on the reading light, leaned back on the propped up pillow, stretched my legs and began to flip through the diary till something interesting arrested my eyes.

Most of the pages of my father's diaries are a recordation of day-to-day family expenses. The amount he earned as his monthly salary, the amount he spent on maintaining his large family and the amount he had deposited as monthly saving in the head post office were all there.

As I found most of the pages of that diary filled with numbers, I riffled through its pages but found no running matter.

Disappointed I put the diary aside, crossed my hands against my chest and tried to go down the memory lane.

What was the last conversation I had with my father before he went into a deep coma and refused to come out of it?

I closed my eyes and tried to recollect. It was about his broken tooth.

My father never used a toothbrush or paste to clean his teeth. His favourite was *neem* twig. At times, he opted for banyan or poovarasu, depending upon the availability. Maybe that is the reason why he had all his teeth in perfect shape and condition.

When we went to gather the remains of my father after the cremation for the milk-sprinkling ceremony, we were surprised to see his jaws unconsumed by fire. Both the jaws held all his 32 white teeth and when my uncle took them in his hands and tapped them on the ground to clear them of the ashes, no tooth preferred to fall out.

"Now I know the value of brushing teeth with twigs," remarked my uncle and laughed. His mouth looked like a dark cave and I could easily count his teeth on the fingers of one hand. Even those few left him soon and his face resembled a ramshackle hut.

"You preferred to use tooth paste while your brother – my father – preferred twigs. Why?" I asked my uncle.

"That's because I am destined to lose all the 32 white terrorists even while alive, while your father's 32 white friends didn't ditch him even after his death," my uncle replied.

"But, uncle," I said, "He has one broken tooth."

"Is it so? Hard to believe. I distinctly remember to have seen all his teeth intact in his jaw bones on the day we collected his remains."

"Your eyes have cheated you. One of his molars is half broken and he has faithfully guarded it in his almirah drawer. I too have not disturbed the relic my father had left."

"Funny! A broken tooth as a relic? Is there a story behind it?"

"Yes, of course. That was the last story my father had narrated to me before he slipped into a coma."

"I see! Sounds interesting... Would you like to share it with me?" My uncle let out a guffaw and that tickled me to an uproarious laughter.

"Stop it sunny! Now go to the story," he insisted.

"You know, my father was in-charge of the general stores of the New Mill," I began.

"Hei! Hei! Hei!" my uncle interrupted and said, "I know all that. Do not try to introduce your father to me. He was after all my own brother, older than me by just five years. Go straight to the story."

"I have to begin somewhere, you know," I said and continued, "Ayudha pooja festival came and my father had had to supervise the cleaning of the entire stores. He told me that it took his six assistants more than six days to do a perfect job of it. It was only when they moved a huge wooden container they came to know that the place was infested with thousands of cockroaches. The abominable creatures began to crawl all over and at some spots they were so many that a couple of assistants began to throw up. And you know my father really hated the pests with a perfect hatred."

"Hei! Hei! Hei!" my uncle said as he shook his head wistfully.

"No! No! No!...Just listen to me. You can only hmm and haw. No more hei...heis," I said, "We are moving with the story."

"Okay then! Go ahead," came the green signal from my uncle.

"I was getting ready for battle," my father said. "The first thing I did was to study the enemy. To know your enemy is half the battle won. I tracked their movements, found out the holes in the huge wooden container through which they entered. One of my assistants made use of his Holmesian brain to detect where they gathered to hold their meetings. I was cunning enough to find out who their leaders were and also their feeding habits. Once the spadework was done, I decided to erase those nasty pests not only from the storehouse but also from the face of the whole earth. At first, I thought of several weapons like the batons to thrash them to death or bait or trap or what not. I was beginning to lose hope as if it were a mission impossible. But then insecticide began to dangle before my mind's eye and it became my first weapon...and the last weapon too."

"Hei! Hei! What have these cockroaches to do with the broken tooth of your father? Are you trying to fool me?" my uncle raised a doubt.

"Please uncle...please hmm and haw. I am taking you to the mystery of the broken tooth. Have patience."

"Hmm...haw..."

"The best way to vanquish one's enemy and emerge victorious is to catch one's enemy by surprise," my father continued. "Insecticide worked like tear gas. I saw with my own eyes a mammoth battalion of cockroaches squirming on their backs, as life painfully oozed out of them. Death dominated the place. I patted my back as I enjoyed watching the pests perish. Victory is sweet."

"Is that the end of one story and the beginning of the other?" questioned my uncle, showing his contempt for the cockroaches.

"No...no...no... How can you expect the end of the story so soon? Listen, uncle, listen. It seemed a second battalion of cockroaches marched out of another hole in the ground, perhaps to wreak vengeance. As my father commanded his subordinates to empty another can of pesticide into the hole, a third battalion marched from yet another hole. My father too joined his helpers in the great attempt to kill every cockroach they came across. One crawled under my father's dhoti and you know how he would have hurled all sorts of expletives at the teasing cockroach, all the time jumping and dancing to the movement of the lonely pest on his body. At last, the cockroach showed mercy on my father and crawled out of him. As if he was waiting for such an opportunity, he brushed the poor creature onto the floor and brought his foot heavily down onto it. Poor thing! It went out of shape. The battle continued and the souls of the cockroaches left the world once and for all."

"Back home," my father said, my dear uncle, "I took a water bath and slipped into the bath tub, scrubbed clean every pore in my body. Yet the stink of cockroaches was still in the air and it was assailing my nostrils. I could not eat on that night.

"After the battle was won, I wanted to take rest. I stretched myself on my cot and sleep embraced me," my father said. "I do not know how long or short I slept, but a sudden feeling of serrated legs climbing on my nose startled me awake. I gave a big punch to my nose and I was sure it was bleeding. However, I was not sure of what was bleeding – the cockroach or my nose. In another moment or so, there were these creepy crawlies all over my writhing body. I slapped my body here and there in an attempt to kill them or drive them out. I hit myself so hard that it became a painful experience. But yet, those detestable creatures have to be done away with.

"The very thought of squashing them and having all that messy stuff on my skin made me want to vomit. It took no time for me to find out what actually created that nausea. A roach comfortably seated on my bushy moustaches was trying to probe into the possibilities of entering one of the live caves close by. It was the stench so close to the nose. Without giving even the slightest jolt to the cockroach, I searched for anything that would swat and kill the adventurer.

"What came in handy was a copper tumbler, half a foot tall and quite heavy. It was half full with drinking water. I gently took the tumbler by its neck, swung it a little and with very great force brought it heavily on my upper lip...bang.

"My perturbed mind was so satisfied that it peacefully lulled me into sleep. Next morning, I woke up and the thought of the roaches began to haunt me all over again. I rushed to the mirror to see what really happened to my upper lip.

"There was no sign of the cockroach and both my lips looked as fit as ever. So, was it a dream? I asked myself. Before I could find any answer, my tongue touched something lying loose inside my mouth. I ran my tongue all over my teeth only to find a part of a tooth missing. I bared my teeth in front of the mirror and found a half tooth sitting tight in the gum. I pushed my right forefinger, thumb into my mouth, and pulled out the other half.

"How did this happen? If it is not a dream, where did the squashed remains of the cockroach go? If it is a dream, how did I break my tooth?" my father lapsed into silence.

I looked at my uncle. He was half asleep. I was not sure if he had listened to the complete story.

"Are you listening, uncle?" I asked.

"What were you saying?" he asked in a daze.

I opened my father's almirah, pulled a drawer, took out the broken tooth and showed it to my uncle.

"Whose tooth is this?" he asked as if unaware of what I was talking about.

"Weren't you listening to the story I narrated?" I asked suspiciously.

"Hmm...haw...Where is the other half of the broken tooth?"

An unusual silence fell between my uncle and me.

I sighed.

□

The Troublemaker

Children are the most loved creatures on Earth till they start loving mischief. A mischievous child is a real menace to its parents and the trouble is all the more if one of the parents is not a home-maker.

There comes a stage in every child's life when its intuition tells it that unless it cries its lungs out, it can't get a drop of milk to drink. There comes another stage when its intuition informs it that it has to play adamant to get things done. It is this adamant attitude that easily passes for mischief.

On such children, parents use a weapon, a four-pronged one at that. They use the prongs one after the other. At first, the parents cajole the child by pouring sweet nothings into its wee ears. The result of such an action would be nothing more than futile.

The second prong is used for the purpose of luring the child with chocolates and biscuits. Very rarely are children attracted for they are in every way aware that such bribes are meant to distract them from their one aim—one desire—one goal.

The third prong is a teaser. Here enters the bogeyman. Sometimes the bald-headed neighbour or a dark-coloured relative would pass for a bogeyman. Such a thought about that unwanted man either silences the child or gives full throttle to its cry.

For those children who howl non-stop and allow their parents' B.P. to shoot up, the last prong comes in handy.

This prong is a thrasher. Parents use this weapon on their tiny tots mercilessly for they are left with no more prongs. It is like a battle. Only one of the two can win.

My story is about a tiny tot who belongs to the category of winners. Once a winner, the child is always the winner. It is only the parents who are destined to fight the losing battle.

Well! To get into the story…

Ramana was pushed into a crèche. His parents, being office goers, couldn't think of any other option.

In the absence of his parents, Ramana's only solace was his grandmother. But she was quite old and so found it difficult to attend to too many chores. When his mischief went beyond compare, she complained to her son of her inability to care for the child all through the day.

The grandmother was aware that Ramana was by nature very curious and it was this curiosity that drove him to all sorts of mischief. She found it hard to answer his fusillade of questions and his questions went non-stop unless she took measures to stop them. She had to do it, though she knew pretty well that the child needed company and was all the time trooping like a colt at her heels.

Once when she was frying fish on the gas stove, Ramana, who was all along pedalling his tricycle in the reception hall of the house, attracted by the sound and fury entered the kitchen.

"Ayah! What are you doing?" he asked in a singsong.

"I am frying fish for you, child," answered the grandma in an affectionate voice.

"What fish, ayah?"

"Pomfret."

"What pomfret, ayah?"

"Black pomfret."

"What black pomfret, ayah?"

Granny was dumbfounded. She searched for an answer and, with great difficult, found one. "Black Pomfret from the sea, child."

"Sea! What sea, ayah?"

"Bay of Bengal, child," granny said. She knew what would be his next question; she also knew that she had no answer for it. And so she grunted, "You are asking too many questions, Ramana. Go and play."

Ramana didn't budge. He waited for his grandma to cool down. He patiently waited. He knew that his patience would be rewarded.

A couple of minutes passed. Granny looked at the child from the corners of her eyes. Ramana noticed her. As she smiled, he burst into a fit of irrepressible mirth, shaking himself violently.

"Ayah! "Ramana cooed.

"Yes, dear!" Granny lifted up the child and sat him on her hip. The moment he was comfortable, he kissed her on the cheek.

"Good boy… goody-goody boy," granny said in all jubiliation.

Ramana, as if he were waiting for such an opportunity, pounced at it. "What is this, ayah?" he asked pointing at the burning gas stove.

"That is a stove, dear," she said.

"What stove, ayah?"

"Gas stove."

"What gas, ayah?"

"Cooking gas, dear."

"What cooking, ayah?"

Granny cocked her head. Her brows were furrowed. "Oh! This fellow is going to start all over again." She mumbled to herself and let the boy slide down her hip to the floor. "I have a lot of things to do. Go and play," she said.

"Okay! I'll leave you to your work. But only if you tell me what this is," said Ramana as he pointed out the knob of the double gas stove.

"That is a knob."

"What knob, ayah?"

Irritated beyond limit, granny grunted, "I do not know what knob that is... I know only its purpose. If you turn it to its left, the oven will burn. Turn it to its right. It will stop... no more questions. Now go and play...I have to wash clothes now...go...go...go."

Ramana disappeared from the kitchen. His grandmother too left the kitchen to wash clothes, while the fillets of fish were simmering on the gas stove.

Washing over, granny hurried back to the kitchen to turn off the burning oven. But it was already turned off. She tried to recollect but her poor memory failed her. "Who would have done this? Definitely not Ramana. He is too tiny to reach for the knob. Only I would have done that," she consoled herself, though an iota of suspicion lingered in her mind.

Granny didn't in the least know that the tiny tot had made use of an easy-to-lift plastic stool to turn off the knob. Her suspicion grew all the more when at the dining table everybody complained of the semi-cooked fish.

"Oh, intolerable, unbearable," yelled granny and said how Ramana made his escape into the backyard of the house and splashed water on dried clothes and on himself. "Oh, I can't even rest my head in the afternoons. I have to keep vigil over the boy."

Ramana's parents, in order to give the old lady the rest she wanted to enjoy in her old age, decided to send the child to a crèche.

Niranjana, Ramana's mother, went around the city to find a suitable crèche for the boy. A three-day search yielded fruit. She found one – a good one at that – very near to the office wherein she worked from morning nine to evening six.

The boy will be away from mischief during that period of time and his grandmother could continue with her household chores undisturbed. Surely she would feel lonely, yet…The boy will be back in the evening and who knows what ideas would assail his head and prepare him for new mischief.

The crèche was only a play school. A huge hall, that could easily pass for a sophisticated godown, made the crèche. Its walls attractively coloured, the crèche lured Ramana, and as he went inside, he found to his joy a couple of rocking horses, a tricycle, a pedaling car, dolls, building sets besides a hundred other playthings. But what really made him jump for joy was the bevy of little girls.

Girls, as usual, outnumbered the boys in the crèche and Ramana found the crèche a heaven on earth. His mother too was pleased to see him as happy as the bunny rabbit on an acre of green grass.

As soon as the boy reached home, he rushed to meet his grandma, who too rushed towards him and picked him up in her arms. "Ah! My little brat! Where did you disappear all these hours?"

Ramana gave her the smile of a man whose mind was not smiling. "Ah! My little ayah! Where did you disappear all these hours? You should go to the crèche to see what a lovely play school it is. Accompany me tomorrow and you will have fine time there with me."

Granny agreed to go. She said so just to please the child. And no one at that moment would have ever thought that the child would take her words to heart.

The morning of the next day proved very crucial to both the child and his mother.

It all started when Niranjana called the child and said, "Now get ready, Ramana."

Ramana, as if not sure of where he was destined, asked his mother, "Where?"

"Where! You don't know? You have to go to the crèche, darling."

"Oh, crèche! I will go," Ramana said with a sense of jubilance. After a pause, he said, "Ayah is also going with me, you know."

Ramana's words sent a shiver down the bones of both his mother and granny. They were sure that the child was going to create a scene.

"Yes! Yes! I am going with you...Now get ready," said granny winking at her daughter-in-law.

"Oh! Your grandma too to the crèche? That is fine... We will take her along. Now you should get ready," said Niranjana and carried him in the crook of her arm to bathe him.

At the dining table, Ramana's granny fed him with idlis and sambar. "You too finish eating, ayah and get ready for the crèche," he cautioned his granny, as he continued to munch.

"It won't take more than two minutes for me to get ready, Ramana. Now you finish eating and put on your shoes," advised granny.

Niranjana kick-started her scooter and got on to the vehicle. She signalled to her son and like a goody-goody boys he occupied the leg space of the scooter and awaited his granny to occupy the pillion seat.

It turned out to be a huge disappointment to Ramana, when his granny waved her hand and his mother accelerated the vehicle.

"Ayah...ayah," Ramana said as he tilted up his head and looked at the helmeted face of his mother.

"Keep quiet, child. You will have playmates and playthings in the crèche," she said.

"Ayah...ayah..." Ramana cried as he looked askance at his mother.

Niranjana kept quiet and concentrated on the road.

"Ayah...ayah...ayah," Ramana began to scream.

Drivers of speeding two-wheelers looked at the yelling child. A few slowed down their vehicles and inquired into the matter. When they were given to understand that it was the unwilling school kid, they smiled at the child and went on their way.

Ramana continued to scream, all the time uttering ayah...ayah...His non-stop screaming attracted the attention of so many who clicked their tongues and went away pitying the child.

"Oh, god! I have to cover yet another two kilometres to reach the crèche. I am afraid the child would swoon because of his incessant screaming." Niranjana said to herself. But she was non-plussed when a police constable on his rounds stopped her.

The constable ignored the mother and looked at the child. "What is the problem, child?" he asked.

"Ayah!" Ramana wept, frightened of the khaki-clad policeman, who looked like a bogeyman to him.

"Don't cry child...don't cry. I am here to help you," the constable combed the child's hair with his fingers, patted his cheeks softly and asked, "What is your name, child?"

"Ramana," the child said and without a moment's hesitation added, "She is taking me away from my ayah."

The constable stared at the child's mother for a while and asked the child," Is she your mother?"

"She is taking me away from my ayah," Ramana repeated with a whimper.

"What is the boy to you?" asked the constable. He had an indescribable air of one who knew the world.

"I am his mother, Sir...I am taking him..."

Before Niranjana could complete the sentence, the constable interrupted her, "Unless you prove that you are his mother, I'll not let you go."

"You ask the child...It's getting late to the crèche and my office as well," she pleaded.

"Ramana! Who is she to you?" the constable asked in a soft voice.

"She is taking me away from my ayah," wailed Ramana and began to sob.

"Stop weeping child," consoled the constable, "You make me weep. I too had a bitter experience like this when I was a child like you. In my case, I was kidnapped by two goondas..."

"No, sir! Why should I kidnap my own child?" asked Niranjana.

"And so, my dear young lady! Do something to prove that you are the mother of this child...Or else I will have to take you to my police station and inquire into the matter in our own way."

Niranjana became panicky. Tears began to fill her eyes and blur her vision. For a moment, she felt that she was turned into a stone. She came back to her senses when Ramana began to pummel her and howl, "Take me back to my ayah."

"Don't waste my time, young lady! Do something before I book you for child kidnapping," the constable's voice was quite stern and intimidating.

Niranjana pulled out her cell phone and dialled her husband and told him of the scene Ramana has created and of her predicament.

"He is coming from his office...It is quite nearby...may take about five minutes," Niranjana said.

"Who?" asked the constable, with a stare of amazement at the disturbed young lady.

"Who else? My husband!" she replied, wiping her tears with the hem of her sari.

"Husband! How do I know that so and so is your husband. He may be an accomplice in child kidnapping. I know that a gang is operating and many children disappear. And only youngsters like you are at the hub of the gang's operations. I can't let you go unless I am convinced," cautioned the constable.

"There he is," Niranjana said and smiled amidst her tears.

Ramana turned his head and saw his father getting down from his car. "Appa! Appa!" he started shouting in all jubilance.

"Constable! This lady is my wife and this troublemaker is our son," said the young man.

"I am ready to believe that you are the kid's father... But how can I believe that she is your wife?" The constable was stupid enough to ask such a question.

Ramana's father pulled out his purse from his pant's pocket and flipped it open.

"No...No....No....I am an honest man. I don't accept bribe," said the constable.

"I won't bribe you...I can't. Just take a look at this little photograph," said the young man.

The constable took a closer look at the photograph and found all the three in it. He clicked his tongue and said, "We are living in an age of computers. How do I know that the photograph that you showed me is not a faked one?"

"Constable! You are trained to doubt all people at all times. But your aged brain fails to co-operate with you," the young man said, as he pulled out his identity card and showed it to the unduly duty-conscious cop.

The constable peered into the card. The next moment he brought his body to attention and saluted him. "Sir!" He said, "Had your wife told me that you are in the Vigilance Department, I would not have stayed her for such a long time."

"You did your duty constable! But use your brain," Ramana's father said, as the constable moved away from the scene he had created.

"Appa! Ice cream...vanila ice cream," shouted Ramana as he jumped into the welcome hands of his father.

"Rare to come across such constables. Let their tribe increase," said Niranjana as she stared into the distance.

□

Afterword

Storytelling has been recognized as a source of entertainment over the years. In addition, it has been viewed as a powerful tool for change and the overall development of an individual's personality and as an effective method to address social issues. Primarily it can bring joy and then it can bring reform. P. Raja generally adopts the former aim. We have always loved a good story and we have always had storytellers. Indians are, no doubt, big on stories. In fact, everyone tells stories in their everyday life. We are just not aware of it. Storytelling is essential to being human. Only by storytelling do we make sense of the world. Animals do not tell stories to each other.

To P. Raja, telling stories seems a natural, inevitable process, like clearing the throat. Perhaps, he can write a short story on the very act of clearing the throat. Life has been all about getting from one day to the next; about surviving rather than living. It provides a writer with lots of opportunities to etch out the vicissitudes of life vividly in words, of course, with a liberal dose of imagination. Rather, there is interplay of imagination and existential experience. P. Raja crafts his stories in such a way that life appears in his short stories in all its vastness and mystery. He writes with no trace of false modesty. The real-life incidents that sneak in are always the things that disturb us enough to wind their way into the space of Raja's stories. True, our daily lives are mostly a mixture of drab routine and unpleasant surprises. However, from time to time, something unexpected happens, which makes life worth living. This is precisely what P. Raja's stories portray. He inhabits a very familiar cosmos and his stories almost always bubble with a socio-cultural undercurrent. He always thinks of people and places familiar to him because that is his own experiential base. Rarely do some stories chart an unknown territory and the reader simply journeys with a certain lesser known reality where ghosts are staring us in the face. His stories, his words, the wonderful characters, offer us the surprise, the excitement, the sense of wonder that kindle the fire of human imagination. All these ingredients the reader can find in all his previous collections of short stories too.

The Black Bitch and Other Stories (2015) is P. Raja's fourth collection of short stories. The other three collections are *The Blood and Other Stories* (1989), *Kozhi Grandpa's Chickens* (1997) and *My Father's Bicycle* (2005). Like his previous collections, *The Black Bitch and Other Stories* presents a kaleidoscope of strange sights and impressions that he observed and felt. This collection comprises twenty three stories most of which were broadcast and later published in newspapers and journals. Here, the meticulously believable and the outrageously fantastical inhabit the world of his short stories.

The first story "A Disease of the Mind" is told in a lighter vein but with an earnest insight into child psychology. When the family breadwinner Vasan pressurizes his wife Seena not to go ahead with her second conception and convinces her to abort it, their daughter Aruna is upset over the absence of a playmate in her own home as Chitra in the neighbour's house has. Two thinkings – one adult and the other child – represent the contraries in life. Of course, life runs by contraries, giving rise to small ironies in life, embodying unexpected turns and twists. Humour is at its best in the ending when the child, Aruna, prays for two playmates much to the embarrassment of her parents.

Revisiting our hoary past packed with interesting myths and tales is nowadays increasingly becoming a trend to contemporize the past and they evoke fresh interpretations emerging from our collective memory, though fossilised but always celebrated for their perennial appeal. Stories like "Ahalya's Curse" can be used to construct a link between events in the past and how we view them today. Ahalya speaks, "Why do you men lose all your senses when it comes to woman?" This question is pertinent even today. She continues, "Sages like you are revered everywhere. People pedestal you in their hearts and worship you. They consider you as an intermediary between God and Man. They think you are wise. Yet how shamelessly you fall for women!" Ahalya speaks thus to the sages in the electronic age too and her words ring true when the press today is flooded with news about holy men indulging in unholy activities. Ahalya is reinvented here as a feminist and advocates the cause of woman: woman is a commodity and "a commodity can never have any opinion of its own." Ahalya is pictured as a chaste woman in her right and modern Ahalya curses the sage who turns into a stone. P. Raja looks at the familiar story through his postmodernist eyes and the story is retold by contextualizing the past in the contemporary with an ironic sting in its tail.

"Pousse-Pousse" is autobiographical and narrates a personal experience in the Pondicherry museum. Museums invariably speak "in silence for the glory of our past." His portrayal is realistic when he says, "Most of the rooms in these museums stink of bat turd, the only thing not known of in history books." Humour and irony interweave and the story stretches itself into a full-length satire about ill-maintained museums in India. Simultaneously it opens a window on the French lifestyle during the colonial rule: "French-men are real gluttons when it comes to wine, women and food. Their women too had their own clandestine ways. It was this white people's insatiable lust for the warmth of human bodies that had created creoles in Pondicherry."

"Beardless Days" is a slice of the writer's college days. He had a fascination for pure white clothes and so took a fancy to the Naval Wing at college. He was required to sport an anchor beard with well-trimmed drooping moustaches. However, there was an option: a clean shaven face – a face without a moustache. Try as he might, he couldn't succeed in growing a beard within the stipulated time, eventually he sacrificed his moustache and it messed up things at home. His mother was shocked to see his clean-shaven face as clean-shaving is part of the obsequies on one's father's demise in Tamil culture. His father was livid with rage and slapped him. The narrator's dream of becoming a Naval Cadet was on the rocks. A real-life incident sneaks in here and the narrator boasts of no false modesty. A drab routine acquires a freshness tempered with lively humour and also with a peep into our socio-cultural undercurrent.

As the title goes, the story "A Day in the Life of a Coolie" records the coolie's activities as entries in a reporter's diary. An actress, who intended to marry a director first, married Bhagavan, a daily wager at harbour and it was the greatest surprise. The director eliminated her in despair. The coolie has stopped talking since then. He takes a glass of hot tea and a bidi as his food for the whole day. He does not let out the smoke, perhaps, to make his stomach burn all through the day to keep his wife's memory alive. P. Raja has the ability to turn a cliché on its head with dark humour and picture in words the existential angst. Life springs unpredictable situations and thereby raises lots of questions. Everybody including the writer is at a loss to answer all the questions. In real life, do we have answers all the time? The dialogic technique with multiple-points-of view is employed here to enhance the coolie's poignant agony.

The story "The Prismatic Pain" opens dramatically and has all the grammar of a good short story. People offer their hair to the gods in temples because generally "they can't afford to offer their hand or thumb." This story is full of laughs and peppered with great wit and satire. "We kids these days are different from the run-of-the mill children," says Sundaram to his father, T. Ramadurai. "God has blessed us with a body and no part of it can be discarded." "You lose a part, you lose your shape. Every shape is divinely," the son echoes his father's words reiterated many a time. The boy checkmates his father when the latter trims his moustaches. Similarly, for a scorpion, its tail is a very important limb. So we have no right to deprive the scorpion of its tail in self-protection. This story emphasizes the balanced ecosystem and God's creations neatly fall in place, albeit his mysterious paradoxes and contraries that make us raise our eyebrows in awe. P. Raja enjoys layering such essential truths in the folds of his stark stories, which deal head-on with philosophical enquiries.

The subsequent story, "Call Yourself a Plant," runs in a similar vein. The special plants on Victoria's house terrace don't bloom even in season. She is upset at their indifference and calls them heartless mercenaries. She has not failed to perform her duty. "Life moves on only when dreams turn into realities. Fizzled out dreams only dart venom-tipped sharp arrows into our craving heart." The middle-aged Victoria has only dreams about babies and her dreams are yet to come true. Pathos is subtly woven into the narration and her despair surfaces through a surrealistic image – the faithless plants. The metaphor of barrenness is an archetypal thing and has incredible reach. You and I can and everyone else can assign to the faithless plants a shared meaning, transcending space and time – a universality of meaning. That the author is talented and profoundly philosophical is borne out by these stories that deserve to be read at leisure and the reader can find something more than the author has planted in it, waiting to be discovered.

Like Ted Hughes' poem "The Thought Fox," the story "The Word Processor" captures the ineffable moment of the arrival of a creative thinking, "No writer worth his salt ever knew or will ever know the vagaries of creative process." Sitting at his PC, he is waiting for "Goddess Saraswathi to come to his rescue, or at least an angel or a devil to descend on him." There is an imaginary interaction between the computer and the author. The computer begins to tell him a story but soon it goes silent, incapacitated by a power cut. The narration sounds like a modern fable marked by a heightened imagination and a keen eye for detail in describing the behaviour of a computer.

In the story "Night Mare," the author's fertile imagination runs riot with luscious descriptions of a queen's concupiscence for an extra-marital affair with one of the palace stablemen – the "night mare" that visits him nocturnally with an arsenal of trickeries in the war of love. King Bartruhari eavesdrops and feels ashamed of his deficiencies in this love war. He runs into an encounter with his conscience and takes lessons from the illicit paramour. He renounces the throne and the queen feels happy that she is "instrumental in making an emperor a sanyasi." However, the credit goes to the stableman, the king says, and instantly quips: "when do you intend to make the stableman another sanyasi?" Such kings, queens, stablemen come and go, but there is nothing for a woman like a ride on a man of her choice – socially licensed or not. When you go microscopic in narration, you create something that has a universal appeal. This story probes into certain eternal complexities in human relationships that defy logic and reason.

"The Wart" is yet another story where the author goes philosophical and talks about persons who survive death through their good deeds. The growth of a wart in Noah's face is God's will and it remains inexplicable and inevitable. But for the wart, Noah is in full shape that others envy. The story has a divine setting and God communicates with a human being. While God tries to justify His ways to man, man tries to question His justifications. The story is biblical in nature and structured to convey a universal truth besides religious overtones: "he who always seeks evil in others finds it." This story illustrates P. Raja's fabulous retelling of a biblical myth and makes the message ever relevant as it penetrates into the consciousness of the writer as an artist and peels layer after layer of some biblical characters. It is revealed that man has not changed much since the days of Noah of the Old Testament.

The story "Compassion" is about the narrator's companions in his study, a large family of mice. Initially he pitied them but when they had feasted on the *Complete Works of Shakespeare* and the twenty-volumes of *The Arabian Nights*, he decided to do away with the mice and succeeded with his spouse's help. After a gap of time, when another mouse made its presence, he felt the absence of his spouse who had left the world by then. The thought of her absence fills his throat and he swallows hard. Despair is rushing to overflow his banks. P. Raja hits peak form as a storyteller here and he is adept at blending humour and pathos while going on and on in such detail. When the readers split their sides with laughter, they are in for a rude shock and a pall of gloom comes over them. We can't but feel a lump in the throat: "who can ever understand the vagaries of fate?"

P. Raja makes abstractions characters in his short stories, and "Suicide" is one where Life is imagined as a character to interact with the protagonist, a famous surgeon, Dr. A. Surya Sundari when she is getting ready to commit suicide by hanging. The noose she has made is the life-snatcher. Life tries to dissuade her: "All confusions arise only to be cleared. Every question has an answer. If a problem fails to find a solution, then it can't be a problem at all." Such effusions gush forth to make the spinster-doctor see reason and read the realities of life. She spurns marriage as the institution of marriage, in her eyes, has floundered across cultures. Still she can develop a relationship by adopting a child. One should shed worries "like a snake that sloughs off its skin." The doctor turns a deaf ear to all these exegeses. Life puzzles her as the last effort by asking, "How do you know that worse things are not waiting for you there?" in the other world after death. These words shake her back into a new awakening and let go of the noose. The author has come up with a novel way of meditating on life and its purpose. LIFE comes with many challenges, the ones that should not scare us are the ones we can take on and take control of. Life is all about getting from one day to the next; about surviving rather than living. On this universal principle lies the essence of the story "Suicide."

In any game, one is bound to win and the other to lose. Rarely do they face a tie. Like a coin that has heads and tails, the spirit of patriotism can be viewed from both the sides across the border between two suspicious nations. One's patriotism is the other's disaster and it is applicable to both the sides. The story "The Sinner" presents one point of view by Father Antonisamy who helped a student in his higher studies. The student is now a scientist who designs war weapons. He does his job and discharges his duties, Karma. *The Bhagwad Gita* also preaches such an ideology and the scientist is right from his perception. Father Antonisamy perceives the scientist as a sinner whereas the scientist holds his head high as a breadwinner and also as a nation builder. The story presents a contrast and such contrasts constitute the rules of life game. Rules are the same but perceptions differ.

Painters and artists rarely care for their external appearance. If painters use brush, writers use pen to paint pictures in words. However, this may not hold true for teacher-cum-writers. The story "Best for the Occasion" explores the unique psychological qualities of a child while stressing the dignified looks of teacher. Impressionistic minds are over-inquisitive and Auro has one. Elders find themselves bowled over when they underestimate the children of today because of inflated self-worth and when their own ways of tackling the young ones boomerang and embarrass them.

Next in the collection is the titular story "The Black Bitch" that shows the author's keen eye for the behavioural patterns of animals, especially the dog here. It is a leaf in the author's career book and a slice of his experience in Karaikal where he worked as a college teacher. The black bitch was a street dog and won't eat in men's presence as she was shy of men. Blackie became his guardian angel. It was pious too and imitated the muezzin coming from the nearby mosque, "standing on its hind legs." The municipal dog-catchers released it, admiring its piety. But Blackie was peevish in the absence of his companions and it behaved differently. Stories like this portray the cultural moorings and establish P. Raja as a master storyteller and a prose stylist.

The story "Sorrow of Sanity" talks about a guilty professor who daren't harm animals like cats and dogs. Accidentally, his car ran over a kitten and his psychological conflict is beautifully brought out. The stories "Ghost Story" and "Penalty" are dipped in popular Indian superstitions. The eerie atmosphere P. Raja creates with his descriptive power effortlessly transports the reader to the world of supernatural so that we have a feel as if we were part of the cast in the strange dramatic encounter between humans and the extraterrestrial. "Penalty" adopts a fable mode to expose certain harsh realities about the pathetic conditions in which childless Hindu women find themselves in the socio-cultural context and thereupon unshed tears gather in the corners of our eyes. Incidentally, a native, folklore-inspired interesting explanation is given for the periodical disappearance of the moon, the scientific reason notwithstanding. P. Raja's art here is that of a miniaturist, dwelling on specifics with a delicate and detailed brush. The story "Nirvana" punctures a loquacious teacher's inflated ego and drives home the message that knowledge has no bounds. A boy who prefers to be self-taught in the company of Nature proves a better teacher than the one trained in a formal learning system. "Sri Aurobindo"s Shoes" captures two great patriots of the pre-Independence era, Sri Aurobindo and Bharathi, the Tamil revolutionary poet, in a single frame and spotlights Sri Aurobindo's poise and serenity as he has no grudge when the latter flicks away a pair of new shoes sent to the former by his brother in Calcutta. Rather he is quick to realize that Bharathi's need for the shoes is greater than his and thereby stands above the rest of human beings.

The stories "The Fun Lover" and "The Troublemaker" deal with an impish boy and are heavily loaded with uproarious fun and laughter. The boy Ramana is over-inquisitive and takes very seriously whatever others say to placate him to the letter and outwits his grandfather-writer who melts before his innocuous innocence and unsullied audacious adventures. The boy ingeniously makes his grandfather oblige his wish of tearing the leaves of a precious dictionary in the writer's study by the owner of the book himself. One day the same boy exasperates his mother in the thick of traffic when she takes him on her scooter to a crèche, by his persistent menacing appeals to everyone to help him get back to his grandmother who casually agreed to accompany him to the crèche early that morning as a truce to start him for the play-school. The duty-bound conscientious traffic policeman assumes the mother to be a child-lifter and threatens to charge her with abduction. It is all fun all the way. P. Raja is a painstaking observer of the on-goings all around and has a penchant for transforming the too familiar into a perennially enjoyable read. The story "The Tooth" is nostalgic and pictures the writer's father as a man of meticulous planner and as a man of convictions to which he holds on by keeping his teeth in tact even beyond his demise and cremation. Such real happenings are adequately coated with imagination and humour, and P. Raja does it with an air. His deft handling of the material on hand transforms every vignette, real or unreal, biographical or historical, into a pure piece of entertaining narrative that pleasantly appeals to both young and old.

P. Raja has been mainly a storyteller of subjective sentiments and personal quests but at the same time he could assimilate into his narrative all that carry a universal impact and transcend time and space through his meditative analyses of human predicaments. He is known for his mischievous humour. To him, a hippo appears "as though shaven by a skilled barber"; a painter from Sri Lanka "was exhibiting her gifts from god in all places of her anatomy."

He draws characters largely from the middle class into which he has been steeped since birth. With a view to capturing the authentic flavour of the situations he describes, he uses the technique of transliteration since literal exactitude in such places does fail to convey the spirit of the Tamil expressions like, *katri veyil* (dog days) *boori kizhangu* (potato curry), *Aayya* (grandmother), *ammavaasai* (New Moon day) and *meenu meenu* (fish, o fish). These expressions effortlessly bring before our mind's eye the cultural ethos and social ambience that form the backdrop in all his stories. Each of the expressions is a pigment of the cultural picture. The key for his narrative is vocabulary, and words come to him un-summoned, and with words he plays all sorts of trickery. A storyteller mastering the short story form, his style was fashioned by his surroundings, his semi-urban environment and the inherited cultural ethos of his forbears. Wit and humour are his forte and these ingredients are always subtly woven into the fabric of his narrative technique, while touching on something profound.

—Dr. D. Gnanasekaran
Former Professor and Head, Dept. of English
Kanchi Mamunivar (Govt.) Centre for PG Studies and Research
Puducherry

□□□